I0717924

IT'S TIME FOR MO

IT'S TIME FOR MO

A NOVEL

RON ANCRUM

Books may be purchased in bulk quantity and/or special sales by contacting the publisher.

Published by Mynd Matters Publishing
715 Peachtree Street NE
Suites 100 & 200
Atlanta, GA 30308
www.myndmatterspublishing.com

978-1-957092-79-9 (pbk)
978-1-957092-80-5 (hdcv)
978-1-957092-81-2 (ebk)

FIRST EDITION

ॐ

This book is dedicated to my mentors.

Bill Trueheart was the University of Connecticut admissions officer when I applied. I learned that we grew up in the same neighborhood of Stamford, CT. Similar to Bill, I worked in college admissions and later in philanthropy. Without his support and encouragement, I would not be where I am today.

Hubie Jones and I first met when he hired me as a consultant in 1993. He was on leave from Boston University to serve as the Interim President at Roxbury Community College. Since then, we have maintained a close friendship. He has been a major inspiration for staying committed to community service and defining what it means to give back.

I would not be who I am without them. You learn from your mentors. They offer the kind of role model that keeps you true to yourself. Everyone needs a mentor guiding them through their life's pathway. Mentoring, at its best, brings about a mutual benefit. I can only hope for the many young people whose lives I have touched over the years that some refer to me as their mentor.

Thank you to my wife, Pam Cross Ancrum, Marita Golden, Ronia Stewart, and Ahmad Blair, for your assistance with writing this book.

ॐ

Contents

CHAPTER 1

Getting the Day Started

Morgan was in a deep sleep when the alarm loudly sounded. He reached over to end the incessant buzzing but his fingers kept missing the right button. He refused to open his eyes even for a moment. *Let me sleep for just a few more minutes*, he thought. That's all he wanted. Maybe ten to fifteen more minutes.

He could faintly hear on the radio:

Good morning listeners. It's going to be a lovely day in the city. The current temperature is forty-five degrees, with a high of seventy this afternoon. Traffic looks excellent at this hour—no reported accidents. In the news overnight, we received a report of two men attacked on the southside. Both were severely beaten and one has a broken nose and concussion. We also have a report from the city's housing department regarding an increase in the number of unhoused citizens and the lack of affordable housing.

Darkness surrounded him as Morgan opened his sore eyes. He blinked a few times before looking over at the alarm clock.

It was six o'clock and no one else in the house seemed to be stirring. He could hear the street noises, cars passing by, a garbage truck picking up cans from the sidewalk, and birds chirping their morning songs. The noises were different from what he was used to hearing. Most days, he would rise from bed around nine o'clock, in time to get to work by noon. By then, the street sounds were that of a busy neighborhood. He had to rise today because it would be like no other day. He was heading to the leasing office at Grace Gardens to sign the final documents that would allow him to move into an apartment he could call home. Yesterday, he received a call from the leasing office that an apartment he had worked hard to get was available for move in. He was ready for this particular moment.

Morgan had turned twenty-two on his last birthday and no longer wanted to be treated as a kid but as a young adult. In his mind, by his age a young man should have his own place to live. After high school graduation, he was left without a plan for what was next—staying around the house with no J-O-B, as his dad would spell it out. As far as his parents were concerned, not working was unacceptable. They would have been happy with him leaving for college, but Morgan did not want any part of that experience. His parents grew up during a period when going to work right out of high school was the norm, if not sooner, and the family expected everyone to contribute to the household expenses. Maggie, his mom, was an office administrator at City Hall. She worked a typical eight-hour day and came home to fix dinner before she could sit down. She never openly complained but also never talked about an exciting day at work.

Louis, Morgan's dad, worked an early morning shift as a

production manager at Whirlpool Corporation. The company had been making appliances, parts, and other gadgets for decades. Some workers had generations of family members work at the company. Being a manager meant having the stamina to withstand the long hours and the demanding stress. He was a proud man. Morgan's parents worked hard and had lofty expectations for him. Their hopes for him were like most other parents when it came to their children. They wanted their child to go to college, earn a degree, and make a lot more money.

Morgan grew up as an only child. He was sometimes lonely, but it had benefits, as he received all their attention. His parents came from small families, producing a few cousins he would see mainly during the holidays and summer.

Morgan stood about five feet nine inches and 170 pounds. He was too small for football or basketball at his school. Those athletes got all the attention and recognition. He excelled on the track team as a 200 and 400-meter runner. He was not a star athlete but won most of the meets in his event.

Academically, Morgan could have been more outstanding. He had a B minus average, and had taken some honors courses, and one AP class in Biology. He was not a social standout in school but an above-average kid. He did not get involved in student government or other after-school clubs. Morgan did not have a job, so he would occasionally engage in volunteer service and help around the house. His church would help feed the elderly who were homebound. In this capacity, he would deliver a box of food items to a senior's home. Miss Gentile was his favorite delivery. She had the nicest house, filled with family photos, and a lovely wrap-around porch with rocking chairs that looked out onto the neighborhood around her home. She would offer him a glass of lemonade and a cookie whenever he stopped by. Morgan thought helping someone in need was better than working at a retail store where most other high school students found work.

Morgan had a small group of friends at Eastside High School. The Watchmen, as they were known to call themselves, always talked about what it would be like after high school, and how they would stay close. But that soon ended when reality set in, and *life* got in the way. Sometimes things happen unexpectedly.

The friend group operated more like a club. Most people thought it was named after the DC Comics characters, but it was a statement saying they would watch out for each other. They had each other's backs. Some of them left for college or, like Morgan, stayed home. Bell went to Temple University in Philadelphia on an athletic scholarship. Unfortunately, in his sophomore year, he got injured, came home, and never returned. Tyler, the brightest of the bunch, completed a degree in Business Management at the state university. Now and again, he and Morgan would see each other on the street and stop to chat briefly about what they did as kids, but they never made plans to stay in touch. Cory stayed home and got a job with a tech company that helped pay for his education at the local community college. He moved into an apartment with his older brother and found new friends at work and college. Bobbie joined the army, was shipped to Afghanistan, and in three months, was shipped back in a coffin. His family was devastated. The Lewis brothers, Dante and Damon, also stayed home but got involved in selling drugs. They were caught, convicted, and sentenced and are currently serving time upstate. None of the Watchmen had kept in touch.

Back then, they would walk around the school together and then hang out somewhere afterward. Some of the guys were big and strong enough to fight if taunted into a confrontation, but Morgan was not one of them. The guys knew they had to look out for their "little" brother.

The group shared the enjoyment of video games, watching sports on TV, and eating out at the local burger joint. When they went to a school dance or a house party, they would show up together, and maybe one or two of them would score with a girl, but Morgan was just not cool enough on most occasions.

Eastside High School was considered the best public school in Benton Harbor, Michigan. Of course, not as good as the school in the twin city across the river in St. Joseph's. Morgan's grandparents migrated there in the mid-1900s to find better economic and educational opportunities. The town had less than 20,000 residents, with over eighty percent of them being Black. The school was known for a high percentage of children graduating and getting accepted into college. The sports teams did well in competition, and other students were recognized for their musical talent. Acclaimed soul singer Nia Holmes and jazz saxophone phenom Grace Collins graduated from this school.

Morgan's small group of friends got to know each other at different times throughout high school. Some were in the same classes, played sports together, attended the same church, and lived in the same neighborhood. None were on the honor roll, in student government, or known for any exceptional leadership skills. The idea was to protect each other from getting picked on by a school bully. Now that they had all graduated, it was obvious they would never be together again. None of the old crew was around for Morgan to hang out with anymore.

Morgan's parents named him after jazz trumpeter Lee Morgan but nicknamed him Mo, not only for his name but also the initials of his full name Morgan Ordell. Morgan's parents were always listening to music, mostly his dad. He loved the music and could tell the musician's background and story. He would sing along with the sounds, as best you can with jazz. His eyes would be closed, fully embracing the vibe. On the other hand, his mom preferred some good ole R&B, which has lyrics to sing along with and meaning. She grew up listening to all that wonderful Motown music from Detroit.

It didn't take long for Morgan to realize he needed to find a solution to his situation. His parents were on his ass about everything, especially asking what he would do with the rest of his life. Things had changed since their younger days as children were more likely to live at home after high school. They did not want to hear that he had decided not to attend college. Neither of them had the opportunity to go to college. Not because they weren't smart enough. It just wasn't affordable. They would have done everything possible to gather the funds, so Morgan would not be denied a chance. He vehemently opposed joining the U.S. Army, Navy, or National Guard. He hated the thought of carrying a weapon and feared the possibility of being shot at. Morgan was good with his hands, could fix things, and had some creative skills. Although he took art classes in high school, in his mind, none of that would lead to a career.

Morgan was struggling with what to do and fulfilling the role of being a Black man. He needed to be more motivated. Regardless, he was often successful in completing whatever he started. It was the getting started part that he resisted. He should have been more outgoing. People he would meet liked him but Morgan perceived himself as a bland person. Therefore, this was his most significant problem. Morgan believed he must become a better version of himself, look good, and talk sharp.

After six months at home with his parents' constant questions, he had to leave even though he had few options. Those first six months at home after graduation were tough. Almost every day, he was asked if he had found a job. He would tell them no, not yet. He had no idea where to look. His lack of a decision led to some very heated arguments. They were on the verge of kicking him out of the house, telling him, "If you live here, you have to work." His parents would tell him over and over again how disappointed they were in him and how much they were willing to support his plans to attend college. Morgan needed time to figure things out. But time was running out, and he had to decide quickly. Unexpectedly, after six months, he agreed to move south to live with other family members to avoid the constant lectures.

After more than three years, he had to confront the real problem. It took time for him to realize the two things in life that were the most important—his happiness and achieving success. It was hard for him to figure out what happiness felt like. Moving into an apartment was the start of that process. It was also hard for him to know what success looked like for him and not based on someone else's viewpoint. His job provided that stability and hope for the future. He learned over the years that his parents were not the problem. Instead, he was the problem. He lacked the motivation to do things that most guys his age were doing. That included working, learning, socializing, and dating. He was unsure what to do with his life but didn't want others to decide for him. But Morgan was stubborn and would not listen to advice. He also did not seek advice from anyone. Since graduating from high school, he entered a period of self-awareness, focusing on his thoughts, emotions, and actions and finally believed he was ready.

CHAPTER 2

Aunt Mae

Mo went to live with Aunt Mae, his mother's sister, and her husband, Uncle T. Their house was in Orange Mound, in the southeast section of Memphis, Tennessee. The neighborhood, well-known for its historical significance, was built by and for African-Americans in the 1890s. It was the soul of the African-American community. A place where businesses thrived and people were self-sufficient. His aunt and uncle moved into the neighborhood after it began a significant revitalization effort and encouraged families to return.

Aunt Mae was a kind, sweet soul who allowed Mo to do whatever he wanted—allowing him that freedom was good and bad. She treated him like a little man, even though he acted like an older teenager. Mae and Maggie were almost complete opposites. Aunt Mae was shorter, slightly heavier, always on the go, and regularly attended church. She was a low-key person who rarely displayed her feelings on her face. His mom, Maggie, was taller, trimmer, and stuck to her routine. She was quick to express her feelings.

Uncle T (everyone else called him Tre, short for Trevor)

was not so gentle and, sometimes, a little too stern, barking out orders. He had served in the military, and from that experience, developed his approach to working with other folks. Everything was a command, never a discussion. However, Mo tolerated the orders because he welcomed the discipline and guidance to keep him more focused on what it meant to be responsible. Uncle T was tall and slim, kept his little afro neat and perfectly shaped, and loved sports. He could talk to you for hours about all the major sports teams. Over the years, he started to look much older than his age. It was a family trait.

Living with relatives was like living at home. However, Mo was able to grow up and figure things out over the last few years. He no longer felt as though he was letting his parents down. Before now, Mo would tell them to stop bugging him. He didn't believe they understood what he was going through. Other times he would say he's working on it and getting it together. But with Aunt Mae and Uncle T, it was different. He would thank them because he appreciated their concern.

It was Aunt Mae's idea that Mo move into their home after listening to her sister complain and vent. They had already raised a daughter that was older and now married. They had the space and thought a new environment would help Mo sort things out. It had taken four years to reach this point, but the time was well spent.

Now he was ready to take the next step, get his own apartment. He had a job and had settled into a simple lifestyle. He had personally changed over the past four years. After three months of job searching and a few interviews, he was hired at the new medical center. His life was filled with work and helping Uncle T around the house with repairs and yard work.

He was learning what it meant to own property. Unfortunately, he did not take any time to develop new friendships. He needed to be more outgoing and purposely meet more people. He also didn't own a car, so going anywhere besides work took a lot of effort. He only went out somewhere once he started dating KeTani.

Mo was maturing. His plans called for being financially responsible for himself. He began thinking more about his future and what he must do to get to where he wanted to be. The job exposed him to career opportunities in the medical health profession that did not require a medical degree. His dreams would require more money than he had or could save with his current job. He was in a good job but learned he would need more education or training to advance. Now that enough time had passed, and he was feeling better about what he was doing, maybe he and his parents could have a meaningful conversation without getting frustrated.

Mo's appointment was at 2 PM, plenty of time to get prepared for whatever would be thrown at him. He was suspicious about whether they would reject his application once they saw that he was Black. They had to know his age and his reported income from work. But he did not fill in the optional question regarding race. Mo was aware of the racism that Black people face when it comes to housing. He was determined not to let that hold him back. To him, he was just another young man trying to make it in this man's world. Regardless, he would be appropriately dressed and on time.

The day would be spent packing up his clothes and personal items. He did not own any furniture or household goods, so he had enlisted KeTani to help him figure out what he needed and where to get it.

KeTani, a trained nurse, was a lovely lady he'd met at work. She lived in an apartment with two friends, Jackie and Jasmin, who had a one-year-old baby. They all grew up together and had a lot in common. She was not officially Mo's girlfriend because he hadn't asked her. Yet, the two were very close. Mo dated a few girls in high school but had no steady, rock-solid girlfriend.

Besides her help buying things for the apartment, Mo had been thinking about whether to ask KeTani if she would like to live together. He hesitated to ask her partly because he didn't want to hear her say no, but he was unsure if he was ready for that level of commitment. The underlying truth was that he was primarily concerned about not having enough money to live on after paying rent. He would need some help, and finding a roommate was on the list. Unfortunately, he had no close friends or anyone else to ask, so he figured, why not ask KeTani.

As he lay in bed, he began to envision what his day would be like. The plan was to sign the lease, purchase the items he needed, and move in. Mo was determined to get an early start and be done by sunset. But first things first, he needed to pick up his check from work to pay for whatever he might purchase. Like most folks, he lived paycheck to paycheck. Fortunately, he knew to put money aside in a savings account for moments like this one.

His credit card might have helped if he had more room on his credit limit. Aunt Mae and Uncle T required that he contribute to the household instead of rent. That made his financial situation a little tighter, but who was he to argue with them? They were kind enough to provide him with shelter and food. Plus, Aunt Mae could get down in the kitchen.

He needed to borrow a vehicle and possibly rent a U-Haul truck to move. Generally, getting around the city was relatively manageable without wheels. He used public transportation to get to and from work. The medical center was on or close to the train and bus services. If he needed a car, Aunt Mae would let him use her white Toyota Corolla. It wasn't fancy but it was reliable.

"Just bring it back in one piece with some gas in the tank," she would say. "Not enough time in the morning to stop for gas."

Mo never asked Uncle T for his ride. He was too particular about every inch of his vehicle.

"Be sure to wash and vacuum the car. No cigarette smoke!" He would shout.

Mo did not smoke, but who is to say a passenger would not? Uncle T had to know precisely where Morgan was going and how long he would use the car.

"Boy, don't bring this car back with a scratch on it. Otherwise, this will be the last time you sit behind that wheel."

That was his method for dispersing discipline and teaching responsibility. Uncle T had a Black Cadillac Escalade, which he kept immaculately clean. Some Black men are notorious for owning and caring for a Caddie. That was Uncle T. That Caddie was his status symbol.

Morgan knew he needed to get out of bed to get the day going. He rolled over, placed his feet on the cold floor, and slowly walked to the bathroom to wash up. Mo was not the neatest person. He had trouble finding the hamper or a hanger so clothes were often stacked and sprawled across his bedroom floor. Finding clean clothes was always a challenge so he just threw on the first pair of sweats he could find.

Mo strolled down the hall and two flights of stairs to the kitchen. Most mornings, no one else would be in the house, but today, Aunt Mae was there to support him if he needed it. She was fixing something hot for him, almost like it would be his last home-cooked meal. It reminded him of how good he had it and what he'd miss.

CHAPTER 3

Call Home

"Can I fix you some eggs and bacon?"

"Sure," Mo replied.

Aunt Mae figured he would need her car, so she handed him the keys. He realized he had planned on using her car but had not asked.

"Thanks," Mo responded.

The meal included home fries, juice, and coffee for a well-rounded breakfast. Aunt Mae was happy for him and, at the same time, worried. She understood how huge a leap this would be for her only nephew. She understood he could not do it alone and needed help, yet Mo was determined.

"Is there anything else I can do?" She asked him.

Mo was short with words and just replied, "No."

Aunt Mae had something else for him. She reached over and grabbed a black pouch off the counter. It was large enough to carry documents in a zipper bag with a combination locking system. She told him Maggie had sent it to her with simple instructions to give it to Mo when he was ready. The time had come. They both wanted to know what was in the bag. What possibly could his parents have sent him and kept as a complete secret? Even Aunt Mae didn't have a clue. She was never told and couldn't look because it was locked.

"I hope you have the combination," she said.

Morgan examined the lock and decided to open it later. Aunt Mae suggested he call his parents to let them know what he was doing. Mo looked at her, but no words came out of his mouth. He knew he should call them but wanted to avoid the conversation until after he moved. He just kept on eating.

He thanked her again for letting him use her car. It'd save time and make it easier to pick up his paycheck. He cleaned his plate, placed it in the sink, and walked back upstairs to his bedroom. Morgan finished getting washed up, found some clean clothes, and got dressed.

The day held great significance. It had taken a while for him to reach this point. It was always within his grasp as long as he did the right things and wasn't impatient. *All good things come to those who wait.*

The burden of calling his parents weighed on his mind. He finally gave in and dialed their number. The phone rang several times. Usually, after two or three rings, the phone was answered by one of his parents. Morgan thought, *Maybe she's not home. What a relief.* Then, just before he disconnected, she picked up.

"Mom," Morgan called out.

"Mo, what a surprise. Is everything all right?" Maggie was startled by his call. He never called home at this hour. As a matter of fact, he rarely called at all.

"I'm doing fine, Mom," he replied. "And, sorry for it being so early in the morning. How are you doing?"

"Doing just fine, baby, and getting ready for work. Dad is almost ready to leave for work."

She asked why he was calling, expecting Mo to have something he needed to ask for. She was hoping he was not in any trouble. He told her he had an appointment with someone to sign his new apartment's lease agreement later that afternoon. Morgan paused to give his mom a second to digest what he had just blurted out.

She calmly said, "That's good, baby." She was pleased he was finally sounding all grown up.

She wished him the best before adding, "God will take care of you. I pray for your well-being daily, son. If this is to be, it will be. How big is the apartment? Will you be by yourself? How far away is it from Mae and Tre?" She asked one question right after the other.

"It's not far," he answered.

"You'll be okay then."

"Thank you, Mom."

Maggie was not sure if he had told her everything he wanted.

"Is there something else, Mo?"

"I guess not," he uttered.

"Be sure to let Mae and Tre know we are so thankful for them taking you in. When you get settled, please send your new address. And try to come to visit when you can. Have a great day, Mo. I'll put Dad on the phone."

He had not asked to speak to his father, but now he couldn't refuse. While he waited for dad's voice on the other end of the line, Morgan was trying to figure out what to make of the call. Did she already know about the apartment? Had Aunt Mae told her? Did she not care? Was she happy or sad? He couldn't tell. Morgan's mom usually wants all the details about everything. Today, it was the opposite. She only asked a few questions and didn't push for explanations. Very unusual.

"Hey Morgan, this is a nice surprise. Great news about the apartment."

Morgan repeated what he'd told his mom but did not share too much. He was not about to ask for anything. This was all his doing. His dad asked about a few financial matters, but the conversation went much better than expected, at least for the first ten minutes. Then it came crashing down.

As expected, his father yelled, "Do you know what the hell you are doing? Have you been saving your money?" His booming voice echoed through the phone line.

Silence hung over the conversation as Morgan thought about what to say next.

"I mean…it's about time. What took so long? I know Tre must be overjoyed with the news. I would be."

His father was always tougher on him than his mother. He had this thing about growing up and becoming a man. Morgan thought for a minute. *What does becoming a man mean anyway?*

In the past, a conversation of this nature would become a full-blown argument. His parents were happy he was working but were still uncertain about his career plans. Working at the City Medical Center sounded like a job, not a profession. If this discussion had been in person, it would have gone on for hours. It's probably the main reason why Morgan had not traveled back home to Benton Harbor. Having a phone conversation was better, but Morgan could still sense some discomfort in his decision-making.

"There's something else you should know."

"What's that, son?" his father replied, thinking he might be further disappointed.

"I have a very close female friend. We've been dating for almost two years. Her name is KeTani."

His dad was happy to hear that news. They never talked about women, dating, sex, or marriage. This was new territory for them.

"We should talk but now isn't be the best time. It would be better to discuss this face-to-face and not on the phone. Have a successful appointment, and take care of yourself."

"Okay. Goodbye, Dad," answered Mo, before hanging up.

Morgan was still surprised by his mother's reaction. He could not get their conversation out of his head. There had to be more she wanted to say. Why didn't he ask her how she felt about it? But he was not seeking her permission or approval. She was correct, he rarely called home to say hello or ask how they were doing. He left home, moved south, and contacted them on special occasions such as holidays and birthdays. He never asked them for anything, and they never made an offer. He loved and appreciated them for how he was raised, but as he got older, it became apparent that he needed to make it independently (with minimal help from them). Morgan expected her to try to talk him out of it, but in retrospect, this is what they all wanted. It just took him a lot more time to reach this point.

Now that the call home was over, he needed to focus on the rest of the day. But he really wanted some advice, guidance, or hand-holding. There's no practice time or cheat sheet for what he was about to do. His parents had done it before. If he had an older sibling who had gone through the process, he could've asked them for help. He regretted not talking about things more with Uncle T. Now it was too late. Today was the day.

All Morgan ever heard was to get a j-o-b to become a man. He realized the limited number of older men he had as role models or mentors. Everyone talked about having one and how important it is for young men to have a good role model. Where was he supposed to get one if not his father? Would he have been better off had he participated in an after-school program? Morgan had some peer support from his friends but only a little. There were always other women around giving advice. Morgan looked to his dad for support and a helpful perspective. But in return he often received demands telling him what to do but not why he should do it.

Other men in the family did not live nearby. Older men were at church but were mainly too old and out of touch. He couldn't remember a Black male teacher in high school. He had one in middle school and while the teacher was one of the best, Morgan couldn't remember discussing anything about manhood. Regardless, the teacher would have been better than all the female teachers he had. What could they say about being or becoming a grown Black man? Black men were not in Morgan's life when he needed them the most. He could identify only one person he could talk to at his job about being a Black man. That person was Old Man Evans. He was the one person at work to spend non-working hours talking about life.

The more he thought about it, the more he wished his dad, or Uncle T for that matter, had said more. His Dad always told it to him straight up, which was exactly what Morgan needed to hear. He always felt the need to give advice, whether Morgan wanted it or not. *Maybe I'll call back later,* Morgan thought.

His dad was old school. He kept things simple and never created unnecessary work for himself. He was a proud man who owned his home and had no debt. He was not big on using credit cards and always carried lots of cash. He could barely use a computer and was skeptical about others stealing his personal information. Similarly, Morgan was determined to do things his way. He did not want to ask his parents for any help. Despite not knowing anything about leasing an apartment, he had mixed feelings about asking for their input.

Morgan never had to pay for food, shelter, or related housing expenses. All he knew was that he wanted his place to live his life the way he wanted, and no one would tell him what to do.

CHAPTER 4

Drive to Work

Morgan was on his way to work to get his check. He jumped into Aunt Mae's car, backed out of the driveway, and started down the road. It should only take him about twenty minutes if there's not much traffic. He started to think about what it meant to be a man and realized that women had mostly raised him. His mom, of course, had always been there. She took him wherever she went—to church, the store, visiting friends, everywhere. His dad was always at work. If a parent needed to come to the school, she was the one.

Morgan ran track but was not revered as a star athlete. His dad never attended his competitions. There were no baseball, football, or basketball games with him sitting in the stands to cheer Morgan on or yell at the refs. There were no PTA meetings for him to attend or go to see him perform in the band or a school play. Morgan did not have music or acting talent. They primarily connected at home. Occasionally, Morgan would be told to help his dad with outside chores that provided some time together, but he was mainly under his mom's wing, like a bird in a tree. Never too far away and within hearing distance, if not her sight.

His parents, Maggie and Louis Ordell, knew each other from high school. They were never in the same classes and hung out in different crowds. A couple of years after high school, they noticed each other at a house party. Louis went over to introduce himself. Maggie vaguely remembered him from school, while he remembered her vividly. She always traveled with a group of other girls. She was considered one of the lovely, dependable girls who would be called on to help organize school activities. But back then, he never approached her even to say hello. For some reason, he finally got the courage. After two years of dating, they decided to get married. There was no exciting romance or story about their relationship, not one they would share. It happened in a regular routine progression. If there was something more, they never talked about it.

They always seemed happy together. Sometimes they would sit quietly in a room. Maggie might be reading a book, and Louis would read a magazine on sports or Black culture. They would watch TV, but mostly, they would gossip about people and talk about how things have changed since they were in school. Both of them acted like they were still young. Most people would look at them and say they were elderly.

One of them would say, "Did you see what Ms. Brown was wearing while walking around the neighborhood? I'm not sure what she was trying to catch other than stares from the brothers on the street. And she got them, too."

"Our neighbor, Mr. White, had surgery yesterday to remove that big knot on his forehead. What was that anyway?"

"I don't know, but it needed to be tended to. Should've

been done years ago."

The one thing they shared was their worry about bills. Together, they had enough money to pay the bills and purchase essential household items. They were essentially working class. They never took a vacation to another country. They only visited places where they could drive. The house was modest, and they lived a lifestyle that fit their home, nothing extravagant.

Friends would provide child care when Maggie needed a backup. She had a few ladies from church who took Morgan in or stayed at the house with him. This left him to figure out what it meant to *become a man*. Morgan had no idea what that looked like or what he had to do.

His mom always told him about how to treat a lady and always respect the elderly.

"Respond with yes or no, ma'am or sir. Say please when asking for something, and never talk back," she would say.

She could not tell Morgan what a man must do or should do among other men, brother to brother. How could she? When Morgan heard other men talk to each other, they rarely were polite and mostly shouted at each other. They often colored their words with f**k this and f**k that, along with a few other choice words. Would his use of swear words make him more of a man? He had not thought much about that and was uncomfortable doing it.

Morgan never showed his emotions for fear of being criticized by others. Better to keep them to himself. He would not ask for help or seek an explanation. From his perspective, it was easier to figure things out alone. Everyone seemed to place more demands on him after graduating high school, as if that was some rite of passage. Morgan had observed that in traditional African rites of passage, one's schooling had nothing to do with reaching manhood. There were other tests and ceremonies. Morgan's idea was simple. He wanted to find a place to live independent of their direct care.

Morgan's dad had his routines, working outside, watching TV, and going to work. Most things stayed the same. He didn't belong to a fraternity or a men's organization like the Masons. Occasionally, he joined Maggie in attending church services. When they were all together, it was usually over a meal. If Morgan needed advice, there was no one to talk with. And yet, his parents had high expectations. He had to progress at his own pace, and that's what he was doing.

Morgan worked at the medical health center as a supply technician responsible for the inspection, assembly, packing, and sterilization preparation of trays and sets for use at the facility. The job did not require a college degree. The center provided the necessary training to perform the work. It was steady work, occasional overtime, and good benefits. After work, he rarely went out to socialize. He was not the kind of guy to drop into a bar by himself. As a result, he would go home, have dinner, then go into his room.

If he wanted to, there were plenty of places in Memphis to check out, including some historical and cultural sites. KeTani grew up here, so she had already seen most of these places and preferred to hang out with Morgan at her apartment. They might go to the movies or dinner, but neither enjoyed the club scene. Morgan instead worked his regular hours as well as overtime when available. He preferred earning a few extra dollars to deposit in his savings account. Working was great.

CHAPTER 5

The J.O.B.

organ pulled into the parking lot to enter the medical center. There was a designated area for employees near the staff and personnel entrance. He pulled into a space and headed toward the glass doors. The area was a separate location from the patient and visitor entrance only used by the employees. The security level was much higher at that entrance. You cannot enter through the doors without proper identification. There was a significant effort to keep unwanted persons from the susceptible areas. They also monitored staff to deter them from stealing medical supplies and drugs.

"Hey, Mo," said Jim, the security guard on duty.

"What's up, Jim," Morgan replied.

"Isn't this your day off? You doing an extra shift, or you miss me?"

Morgan smiled at Jim's attempt at humor. He would be the last person Morgan would have missed. Jim looked at Morgan's ID badge and checked the metal detector.

"Have a blessed day, brother," Jim would generally express his feelings about a political topic or race relations.

He spent a lot of time reading and listening to the news all day, especially some of the conservative talk shows. If the police shot a Black man, he would be outraged by the act. When a Black politician was caught in a scandal, Jim would say he never trusted him. Morgan kept moving because he did not have time to hear one of those news stories or Jim's commentary.

Morgan headed straight for the Personnel Office to pick up his check. The office was on the main level, close to the lobby. He remembered his first trip there when he applied for the job. He sought employment at the medical center because everyone Morgan talked to said there were many available jobs. The City Medical Center (CMC) just opened a new section that doubled the size, and they needed more staff at all levels. Morgan did not have any medical or health training, but there were a few jobs for high school graduates willing and able to learn. At least, that's what he'd heard.

The same day he completed the application, they had him take tests. One was to check his aptitude, and the other was to assess his personality. The employment forms were long as hell, asking questions about his past education, past employment, for which there was not much to mention, and his health. Then, they had him sit with a hiring specialist for an interview. Morgan tried his hardest to make a good impression, paying close attention to his words and being positive. If he was to stay, he had to get a job. Working was essential.

Regarding jobs, Morgan's dad had a lot to say. That's all he ever talked about. He would moan about work almost every evening, especially after a drink. Louis would complain about how the company treated him after working there for decades. He would have left if the position did not come with a full pension after thirty years. Louis would call his boss a jerk, and as the top manager, he did not know how things worked.

"If it weren't for me, the place would fall apart. Son, it's extra tough out here for a Black man. We always get the shaft. The man will hire us for menial jobs, low wages, and then give us a hard way to go."

Morgan had never seen anyone so unhappy. His dad would go to work, come home, and after dinner, he would watch TV and go to bed early so he could do it all over again.

"Son, you better get a college education so you don't have to be a laborer and work for 'the man' like me."

He would tell Morgan over and over, "Go to college and become the CEO of your own business."

Morgan did not follow his instructions. Morgan's decision not to go to college led to many arguments throughout his senior year of high school. Some nights, it would spoil dinner. His father was disappointed that Morgan could not figure out what he wanted to be. Louis felt the world was open to becoming anything you want: a doctor, a lawyer, work in high technology, or a bank. There are plenty of opportunities, just pick one and work hard. Morgan was not sure about any of those professions for himself. He had no idea what to major in, what to study, or what school to attend. To Morgan, it would have been a waste of time and money.

One night, Louis was so upset with Morgan that his yelling had Maggie step in between them to protect her child. For months, they did not speak to each other.

Morgan found work at a large organization in a job where he felt appreciated. He does what he is told and does his best doing it. The job, at least, helps put money in his pocket and provides a means for saving. He'd learned some skills from the position but could see himself advancing if he started taking a few college courses. Supervisors at the medical center were always encouraging him to do more. It'd been more than three years in the same position, and they don't like staff to get stuck in the same old job. There were plenty of lab technician positions across the center. Morgan would need to pick an area and take suitable courses.

He recalled his dad's rants.

"You can't be a man with no job."

One day, Morgan and his dad debated the importance of a college degree. The data reported that those with a college degree earned higher salaries. Morgan reminded him that's not always true. Some college graduates found it disappointing to earn less than a plumber, electrician, barber, or owner of a coffee shop. The question should be, what is more gratifying? He wanted to work in a job where he enjoyed what he was doing, and where he could appreciate how others benefitted from the services provided.

His dad mostly believed in ownership and possessions.

"To be a man, you must own your home," he would say.

Louis forgot that mothers also had a role to play in homeownership. He never acknowledged his wife's contributions. He always talked about how he did this and that. She would not say much. Her interest in how Morgan matured was more fundamental. Don't get into trouble, be kind and respectful to others, and find something to do. His mom would be happier if she could get Morgan to attend church sometimes. She believed the Lord would protect him and help him find a job.

Morgan was a good fit for his job. He got along with the doctors, nurses, administrative staff, and other clinical staff. He prepared the medical tools and supplies for use by the physicians. Morgan primarily worked with cardiologists. But, when they were not busy, he might shift to helping in the hospital pharmacy. Mainly, he kept the supplies well stocked, the tools sterile, and the area clean.

In the first few months, he received job training from senior staff. He learned how to sterilize supplies, which tools were used, and for what purpose. He would assist with checking the packaging of the medical products received. After six months, he studied to take the CRCST certification exam and passed. His salary had increased to $55,000 annually. Aunt Mae and Uncle T were pleased. Why not? He gave them $500 a month. His paycheck would go directly into his bank account, primarily savings. If he continued to advance, his salary could earn him as much as $85,000. Morgan liked being in this environment, where so many people did different things but were all connected to help those needing medical attention. It took time to find this job. It required him to be in the right place at the right time.

Morgan went to the Personnel Office to pick up his check, but the person at the front desk could not find it.

"It was placed in a pile of inter-office mail to be sent out. It should be in your mailbox," someone said from a nearby office.

The associate director, who had interviewed Morgan a few years ago, stuck her head out of her office.

"Is that Morgan?" she asked.

"Yes, ma'am," Morgan replied.

The staff person continued, "I have some bad news. The leasing company called to verify your employment. I told the woman you didn't work here."

She looked at Morgan for a reaction.

"Just kidding," the assistant admitted before he could say a word. "Moving into an apartment?"

"Yes, ma'am,"

He did not find her joking around funny. All he could do was shake his head. Morgan did not want to discuss this with her at all.

"Thank you, ma'am, for taking care of that." Morgan left as quickly as possible and went down to the staff mailboxes. Inside was a bunch of old paper and an envelope with his paycheck.

"Got it," he said to himself.

Walking around the building, he passed other staff he knew or had seen many times. Most of the staff around the medical center were friendly. In his workplace, getting to know other staff and building a positive relationship was a good idea. But the place was so big that meeting people made it difficult to know more than a few staff members. As he passed by, he would give them a nod, a smile, and keep moving. But his actions made a difference for the few he worked with directly. With that in mind, he could not just walk into the building and not say hello because then they would talk about him behind his back. Morgan took a quick spin around the O.R. wing. There were workstations where they prepped for surgeries, and the team members paused to take a break. Most of the staff was be there.

Standing around were Tim, Lila, and Charlene. Like

Morgan, they were all between twenty and thirty years old. They all had studied to work in the health field, but not Morgan.

"Hey y'all," said Morgan.

They each responded in their own way.

"We didn't expect to see you today. Putting in some extra hours?" asked Tim.

"No, man. Just a quick stop by the Personnel Office." Morgan replied.

He also did not discuss his plans to move into an apartment with any other staff. They were his coworkers. They were not what he would call friends. They continued to chat for a few minutes socially, and one by one they left to get back to work. Morgan was now free to move on.

His next stop was to see Old Man Evans. This dude was a carryover from the old hospital and was nearly seventy years old. They probably kept him on to receive his retirement, never thinking he would keep working. Morgan appreciated him because he took him under his wing and shared lessons for being a man.

"Hey Mr. Evans," Morgan would say. Morgan didn't know his first name. He always greeted him with mister or "old man."

"Hey Mo," he would say. "What's crackin' youngblood?"

Morgan let him know that today was the day he was getting the apartment. Morgan was proud of himself.

"That's good news, Mo, well deserving. One step at a time," he chuckled.

Morgan remembered the first time they met. He was lifting some large boxes with medical supplies. Old Man Evans came over and said, "Stop, young man."

He let Morgan know he would hurt himself doing it the way he was doing it. Morgan had no idea what he was talking about. The older frail looking man reached down to demonstrate how it should be done. He could not have weighed more than 160 lbs.

"Get your legs under it and get down low. Don't bend over."

He was adamant about not hurting his back. If not today, then surely, as he got older, Morgan's method would lead to back pain. From that day on, the two would chat over coffee breaks. He had some wild stories about work to tell. But what was more relevant was that this "old man" would ask Morgan questions about what he was doing at the hospital and why he had not gone to college.

He had a way of listening. He never challenged Morgan's answers. He would nod his head to indicate his affirmation. Other times he would ask another question to ascertain more information. He would always end a conversation with some form of encouragement. He never really talked down to Morgan or about himself, but you knew he had life lessons to share. He was indeed a mentor.

Over the past three years, Morgan learned more about the "old man." He had been in the Navy, studied sciences in college, mainly worked in research, and worked at the medical center for decades. He was an institution. Old Man Evans had an office in a part of the hospital where few others worked. Morgan was not sure if he had a boss. He just did his thing, and nobody bothered him. Sometimes, they would meet in the café area for tea, not coffee. He would tell Morgan to work hard and continue his education or training to develop his skills.

Always have a plan and never let his dreams dissolve. He was the one who encouraged him to invite KeTani out on a date.

In the past, Old Man Evans was a hospital services administrator primarily working with the human services counseling staff. Morgan would tell him, *One day, I want to grow up and be just like you.* Morgan would eventually need to get an advanced degree to make that happen. That possibility was not far from his mind now that he had been in the real world. Morgan could work here and attend community college part-time. The medical center has an education attainment benefit that provides tuition reimbursement. He would need to be enrolled in a health-related degree program to be eligible.

That morning, Old Man Evans had a slight cough and appeared tired, as if he had not gotten enough sleep. Morgan did not think much of it, but asked him if he was okay. Old Man Evans said he was good. Morgan thanked him for his support. He always enjoyed talking with him about things going on in his life.

"You're the only one who seems to listen and care."

No matter the subject, Old Man Evans understood where Morgan came from and would offer some words of wisdom, more like the truth. Old Man Evans wanted to share some important information but thought he would wait until the next time they were together. He gave him a salute and smiled at Mo. "Have a great day."

Before leaving the hospital, he must stop to see KeTani. He reached for his phone and sent a text message.

A few seconds passed before his phone sounded.

The café was on the second floor, above the lobby. It was a place for staff and visitors to grab a bite. It had sandwiches, hamburgers, other grilled food, assorted beverages, and sweets. After five o'clock, they would offer three different hot dishes. When Morgan worked late, he would have dinner here instead of waiting until he arrived home.

KeTani was sitting in the far corner, their usual quiet place.

"Hey beautiful," Morgan said enthusiastically. "Today is the day."

"Hey handsome," KeTani said in response.

They always greeted each other this way. Like contestants on the show Wheel of Fortune, they always referred to their significant other in these terms of endearment. KeTani knew he was very excited about getting an apartment, a place to call his own. She was excited for him but also a little worried. Since she was already living in an apartment, she understood what he was about to experience. There would be unexpected bills, appliance repairs, and worry about security, to name a few. Regardless, this would provide a place where the two of them, just the two of them, could be together.

KeTani asked, "Did you get your check?"

"Yep," Morgan replied.

Morgan asked her how things were going at work.

"Same old stuff, very busy, somewhat hectic. The bosses are frantically running around. It's hard to tell if there's something special or a crisis."

She stayed clear of it. Morgan paused and then spoke.

"I've been thinking."

"About what?" KeTani said.

"Why don't you move into the apartment with me."

"What? Why would I do that? I already live in an apartment. Plus, that would put my roommates in a bind."

She thought it would take a long time to find a replacement. Also, she was not interested in increasing her costs. She wished they'd talked about this before now. That would have given her more time to decide if it was a good idea, make plans, and everything. KeTani realized her response was not what Mo expected and might have been too harsh on him. She let him know she appreciated being asked. But it caught her by surprise. She needed time to think about it.

Morgan was trying to figure out how he should respond to her. He made sure she understood how much he loved her. After saying that, he immediately thought he shouldn't have done that, worrying it might push her away. He loved her, but he had never said it before and maybe it was not the right moment. They'd been dating for over three years, and he never told her how much he cared for her. She was the only person he dated, and finding time for them to be together without others being around was hard. They worked during the day, sometimes on different shifts. When not at work, they're either at his aunt and uncle's or her place with her roommates and sometimes their boyfriends. He explained how much he wanted to have more time together. He had been thinking about it for some time but never told her.

Morgan stated how much the move meant to him. Once he decided, he asked for her help finding furniture and items in the kitchen. He had never done this before, and she was the only person he could turn to for help. It was the right step for him. He wanted her to be with him. KeTani was pleased he was interested, but it caught her off guard.

"Yes, you're moving, but that was not *us* moving. I'm happy for you and looking forward to spending time with you at *your* place, but that does not translate into *our* place."

She wanted to know if Morgan had any other surprises.

"So, you love me, huh?" Whether he knew it or not, she was picking up on everything—even the words not said. "Morgan, let's just focus on your move for right now."

She promised to give it some thought. Morgan had little choice.

"Okay, take your time," he said.

He'd hoped for an immediate affirmation. He had to give her the space to think about it, but at least he'd asked. If not KeTani, who would he get to be a roommate? He didn't know many people or have other close friends.

Morgan began thinking he needed to leave to cash his paycheck at the bank. He asked if she was okay to go with him at 1:00 PM She answered that she was good. She was hoping he was not upset with her.

It did not go as well as Morgan had hoped. He realized he should have asked her sooner and expected she would want to consider all the ramifications, starting with her parents, who helped support her. She not only had rent to pay but also her college loan. What was he thinking? That was it, he was not thinking. Morgan got up and left the table feeling dejected.

CHAPTER 6

KeTani

organ could easily remember the first time he saw KeTani at the hospital. He told himself he wanted to know her. She was gorgeous. Morgan had met a few other brothers and sisters who worked throughout the medical center but none like her. Most of them were friendly. Only some he considered friends to hang out with outside of work. She instantly caught his attention. Without knowing anything about her, he was focused on finding out which department she was assigned to or when she took her work breaks. Going to the café at the medical center was where he could more likely find the opportunity to talk. In his mind, he was beginning to act like a stalker, and that was not how he wanted to come across.

She wore scrubs that sometimes had a pattern on them. The doctors wore white jackets, and the medical technicians wore blue. Therefore, she was more than likely a nurse. She probably came to the café for lunch if she worked the first shift. This meant he needed to stop there after checking in to his department. One day, he finally saw her again. He walked over and asked if he could join her. She said yes, then smiled, almost to suggest she was pleased he was interested in meeting her.

Her long-braided hair was wrapped and piled on her head. She wore some makeup, not too much, to accentuate her facial beauty. KeTani was about 5" 7" and slender. It was easy to see that she lifted some weights to build strength in her arms to lift patients. Her skin tone was medium brown, with sparkling brown eyes and a beaming smile. Before meeting her, he had not seen anyone else that looked this good all the time, no matter what time of day.

He remembered introducing himself.

"I'm Morgan, but everyone calls me Mo."

"Okay, my name is KeTani."

She did not offer a nickname. They talked for as long as possible, and both left, hoping to see each other again. After weeks of having their café run-ins, Morgan finally dared to ask KeTani out on a date, and they had not stopped dating since then. The relationship was somewhat rocky at first. Morgan was not experienced with dating and having a steady relationship. It was like on-the-job training. KeTani had been in several relationships before, which was her reason for not getting in too deep, too fast. She had too many disappointments with men who mistreated her, cheated on her, and did not give her the respect she wanted. Together, they found a way to be involved and not make a big deal about it. Morgan grew into a relationship that felt safe, and no one got hurt.

She grew up in Memphis and never lived anywhere else. She attended the local college to earn her nursing degree and, until a few years ago, lived at home with her father. Her mother passed away when she was in high school, losing a year-long battle with cancer. Her father remarried, and KeTani didn't enjoy the relationship with her stepmother. The bad relationship caused her to move out of the house and into an apartment with two other friends, Jackie and Jasmin.

It's incredible how they all grew up together but developed different personalities. They were far from being "birds of a feather that flock together." The J-girls, as Morgan called them, each had boyfriends.

Jackie's dude was all right. He worked through law school and had little time to lay around the apartment. He spent most of his time studying. His demeanor was serious and hard-working, and he loved debating any topic. This was his method for practicing to be a lawyer.

Jasmin's boyfriend was very different. He is the father of her child, but for whatever reason, they decided not to get married or live together. They stay at each other's apartments, whichever is most convenient. He worked at the local radio station in the advertising and sales department and had the gift of gab. He was very smooth and charming.

Morgan was not like either of them. They were local to the area, and Morgan was the outsider from up North. They had nothing in common, from what they watched on TV to the music they enjoyed. Things were always cordial between them, but that was it. They never went out as a group.

The relationship between Morgan and KeTani had always been to enjoy each other. Neither one put pressure on the other. They would go out but always slept at their respective homes. This does not mean they did not have intimate moments. They enjoyed going to the movies, eating out, and attending concerts or nightclubs to listen to music. When they stayed indoors, they watched TV. Morgan watched sporting events when the other two guys were around, but that was all he did with them.

When they would cuddle up, their embrace was strong. One of them would turn on the CD player to play one of the old R&B or hip-hop standards. Morgan liked mostly R&B and favored Marvin Gaye. The *Sexual Healing* album was his favorite for these moments. KeTani always preferred Whitney Houston's *Saving All My Love for You*. She had this unique voice, always singing the words as if Whitney needed help. Whatever they played was to cover up the noises they would make when having sex. At first, this was a concern since Morgan entered the relationship as a virgin. He was getting more on-the-job training.

Today was the first time Morgan had discussed the idea of them living together. KeTani looked at him as if wondering where the idea had come from. Her immediate response was no, no way. She didn't want to ruin what they have. Now he realized he should not have waited until the last minute and worked on it gradually. That was a big mistake. Living together was not about building a stronger relationship but making it easier to be with each other. Neither was ready for marriage nor was it about trying to test the waters to decide if living together would work. The biggest mistake was Morgan's lack of understanding of how KeTani felt about him and whether she was thinking about something more. He had not thought about her preference.

They both agreed that living together as an unmarried couple can be difficult. If marriage and having children were outside the plans, questions about the commitment level would arise. If marriage and children are in the plan, you must make arrangements for who does what in the household. Both of these require time, and Morgan provided none. All he could do now was wait for her answer. She enjoyed being a nurse and wanted to maintain her chances of being promoted to the next level.

Morgan began thinking about how Mr. Kenneth Mason, KeTani's father, would react to his daughter's decision to live with him. As often as they spoke to each other, Mr. Mason had always been a little standoffish, not showing any interest in what Morgan did and how he felt about things. Morgan imagined Mr. Mason might not care on the one hand and be adamantly opposed to the idea on the other. As a father, he would think his daughter was pregnant already or the two of them were planning a wedding soon. Neither of these were true. KeTani did not need her father's approval and probably would not ask for permission. She would tell him and hope he didn't do anything irrational.

She needed time to think about it, so he would do precisely that and give her time. Renting an apartment would be better financially for Morgan with a roommate, but he could not identify anyone else he already knew. Sharing an apartment with a stranger was not an option. Morgan had to figure out what would get her to make what he believed was the right decision—moving in together.

He could not get KeTani off his mind as he returned to his car. He told everyone who asked him about his "girl" that she was the loveliest person he knew. They had been dating for about three years. Morgan referred to her as his girl because he was not interested in anyone else. She had never said the same to him. He just made that assumption. Maybe she dated other guys. He dared not ask. Morgan could not imagine her seeing other men. When would she have time? Maybe he needed to pay more attention. Now that he had introduced the idea, he had to wait for an answer.

CHAPTER 7

The Bank

Morgan drove to the bank. As always, Aunt Mae had preset the radio to her favorite R&B oldies show. It was not his first choice to listen to, but he didn't mind. After all, it was her car. *For the Love of Money* by the O'Jays started playing, and he smiled at the coincidence. Today, he just needed his cash in case of unexpected expenses.

As Morgan drove, he thought about his move south. He was pleased that he had a job with decent pay. He was worried about finding something that would provide enough money and not require him to go to college. He couldn't see himself doing what his dad did at the manufacturing plant. That was pure labor, very routine, and nothing creative. Uncle T's job was not much better. He worked for the city in the highway department, ensuring the roads were well maintained. None of that was for Morgan.

Moving south to live with a family member was easy for his parents to accept, plus it accomplished the main goal: getting Morgan out of their house. Living with a family member made it more acceptable than moving somewhere else where he did not know anyone. The move was easy. All he had were clothes.

Morgan took the train to Nashville, then boarded a Greyhound bus to take him the rest of the way.

The adjustment was easy. He was familiar with the house from past visits and knew the family members. But it was a little different when he moved down. Morgan was there to stay. The routines were different, as well as the habits of his aunt and uncle. He had his bedroom on the top floor. When it was time to eat or watch TV, he was with his new family downstairs. Mostly, they left him alone, and he kept to himself. As a person from the North, everything seemed to move slower in the South. However, the people seemed less anxious, more patient, and inherently polite. The expectation of finding what he might do for the rest of his life was now possible in a new, less stressful, environment.

Memphis was so different. He did not know anyone else besides his aunt and uncle. At first, going out to a club or community event took too much effort. He could do a few things once he got the job and met a few people. Regardless, Morgan usually preferred to be somewhere other than where there were crowds. Meeting KeTani provided one person he truly enjoyed being with.

As a southern city, the urban center was smaller, and places were more spread out. With no car, getting from point A to point B was always challenging. He mainly used the local bus service or a ride-share app, if necessary. Most of the time, his race or gender did not matter, but racism and bigotry were always present no matter what the circumstances. He worried about being stopped by the police, about store clerks closely watching him as he browsed merchandise in the store. He would worry whenever he found himself in a situation where he was the only black or brown face in the room. Morgan was more comfortable in a diverse environment. Being in the South, with its history, made him think about what might happen, particularly in Memphis.

When his family talked about the "old days," there were stories of segregated schools and Black only businesses. They kept their thoughts to themselves and stayed away from the white neighborhoods unless it was to go to work for a family. Back then, Black men got pulled over by the police for things they had nothing to do with. Morgan realized some things had not changed. One thing was for sure, folks in Memphis love to eat. Not that up North was any different, but it's the difference between like to eat and *love to eat* here. Good food at restaurants was in abundance. Morgan always felt comfortable when he stopped in a place to grab a bite. Southern cooking was not segregated by race or economics.

Morgan arrived at the bank a little later than he had envisioned but still early enough to achieve all he had planned for the day. The parking lot was half full, which meant a long line at the counter. He spotted an open space close to the entrance, but another driver pulled in just before he reached it. He drove to another spot a few rows away, parked, and hurried inside.

Since he started working, he had deposited a percentage of his paycheck into a savings account every week. Managing money has always been one of Morgan's strengths. He had saved almost fifteen thousand dollars and was prepared to move out. He was grateful to his family for taking him in. Morgan understood that moving into an apartment would now cost much more money. He was uncertain whether he was financially ready but knew it was mentally long overdue.

He had not been at the bank since he opened the account three years ago. Doing business with the bank primarily meant using the ATMs. His paychecks were deposited directly. But for the move, he wanted to deposit his check and make a substantial withdrawal in case having cash on hand might be handy.

Morgan got in line to cash the check. There were at least five people ahead of him and only one teller. After twenty minutes, he approached the counter. The teller looked at the check as if to inspect it for being fraudulent. Then she glared at the computer screen to make sure it was the correct account, and there were sufficient funds. She then asked for a picture ID and bank account information.

"Do you have your PIN?"

Morgan replied with the information.

"What is your birth date?"

He gave her the information and waited for her next security question. Morgan looked at the unpleasant middle-aged white woman, wondering if her demeanor was because she did not want to help him.

After several minutes, the teller said Morgan had to see one of the customer service representatives to get approval. Morgan asked if something was wrong. She said no, just part of the procedure. He also told her he needed a bank check for a specific amount.

"They can help you," she stated and pointed in a different direction.

Morgan was distraught after he waited in line to be told to wait some more. He left the teller's counter and stood close to one of the offices. The lady sitting at her desk was Black with a really nice hairstyle and a fair complexion.

"Take a seat, and someone will be with you shortly," she said politely.

That's when he realized things would take much longer than planned. More than thirty minutes had passed, and he was still waiting to be served.

Morgan looked around the room at the other customers waiting to talk to a representative or standing in the line he had left. A few business folks were getting cash before opening the business for the day. There was also an elderly couple and a lady who looked like she was about to explode angrily. She kept making grunt noises to show her displeasure in having to wait. She sucked her teeth so many times that he wondered what kind of mint candy she was working around in her mouth. Morgan was trying to understand why it was taking so long. The last time he had done business in the bank, it went quickly. All of this was beginning to feel unusual.

After another ten minutes of waiting, the lady in the office approached him.

"How can I help you?"

Morgan said he wanted to deposit his paycheck and make a withdrawal. She asked the usual questions about whether he had gone to the teller. Morgan said yes and that he was directed to the customer representatives. She asked to see his ID. She gazed at it. Then she asked for his account number. Again, he responded. Her tone was always professional, referring to him as Mr. Ordell. He handed her the deposit slip.

"You know, with the online app, you can make this deposit yourself."

"Was there anything wrong with the check?" he asked.

"No, it appears to be fine." She went on to explain, "Keep in mind that a withdrawal of this amount can take up to three days to clear in your account."

"What?!" shouted Morgan. "Isn't a check good immediately?"

"Not really, Mr. Ordell," she explained. "When it's sent electronically, the check arrives, and it goes through processing within one business day. However, with a physical check from your employer, the processing time is typically three days."

With exasperation, Morgan said, "You're telling me it would have been better for the hospital to send the check than for me to deposit it myself?"

"Uh, yes, that's right. You can deposit the check and take a $500 withdrawal if you like."

"Sure, that would be okay."

Morgan also requested that a bank check for $1,900 be withdrawn from his savings account. She did not ask what it was for, but he said it was for a rental lease, and he needed to pay the deposit and the first month's rent. The representative looked at his account again and said she would be right back. Five minutes later, she returned to her desk with a check for the amount he had requested.

"Please sign here," she asked.

After he signed and dated the document, she said, "You should be all set. Anything else?"

"No. Thank you."

He was glad to get out of the bank. Morgan felt he had wasted a trip other than getting the crucial bank check. He probably did not need to drive to the medical center other than to see KeTani. He now had $500 in cash. If necessary, he could write a check and hope they wouldn't try to deposit it the same day. He had more funds in the savings account to transfer into the checking account if necessary.

Morgan returned to the car and sat there wondering if getting the apartment was still a good idea. Was he ready to take such a big step, or was he not being honest with himself? He had saved his money and had no other bills like others he knew. There was no college loan or car payments, and up to that moment, no rent to pay if you don't count the monthly payments to his relatives. He was getting a little nervous.

Getting help with the rent would be nice, which brought him back to why finding a roommate was necessary. He was committed to making the situation work for as long as possible with his savings.

He decided to go back home and start packing. He realized he might not be moving today. He had yet to find a bed. He needed to be ready in case it all came together.

When he arrived in Memphis a few years ago, Morgan didn't have many possessions. Only two suitcases. Since then, he has purchased more clothes and a CD player. He did not have any furniture, nothing at all. Until now, he did not need any of that stuff. *I should have started putting my clothes and personal items in boxes before today.*

He stared the engine, hoping the rest of the day would go much smoother.

CHAPTER 8

Bell

The radio news reporter said,

The weather remains mild today. Later, we hope to get an update on the Southside shootings. The mayor will address the recent scandal at the Board of Education. Tonight, on TNT, perennial rivals the Celtics and Lakers. News brought to you from USA Mutual Insurance. Now, back to Soul Explosion.

As Morgan drove down the street, he noticed a man standing on the street corner with a sign asking for help, which translated into begging for money. He could never understand how a person's life could get to a point where panhandling became the day-after-day activity.

It must be horrible and demoralizing. The homeless man was in regular-looking clothes but wrinkled and dirty. He thought the man on the corner must not have access to a washing machine, dryer, and ironing board to keep himself from appearing disheveled. As Morgan got closer, he looked over and realized it was a familiar face.

Oh my, he looks like Bell from back home. Morgan thought

that couldn't be true. Bell, here in Memphis, begging for money? As he drove past him, he saw a car had pull up and someone handed the man what looked like a few dollars. Up to this point, Morgan had not stopped.

Of all the old gang, Bell was the one that had it made. He was a star high school athlete, recruited to play at the collegiate level, and destined to be drafted into the pros. Suddenly, it dawned on Morgan again that Bell was not supposed to be in this city, not here, especially on a street corner begging for money. If it is him, why was he here?

It can't be. Isn't Bell back home?

Morgan drove about a half mile after he passed him, then stopped after a couple of blocks. Morgan decided to turn around. How could he drive past him like that, as if he didn't matter?

Morgan did a U-turn as soon as possible and drove back to where he spotted Bell. Morgan pulled up alongside him.

"Get in!"

Bell looked in the car window at the man who just gave him an order, and to his astonishment, it was Mo, his homeboy. "Get in," Mo said again. "Let's go somewhere and grab something to eat. I can't leave you out here on the street."

Bell just stared but had a slight smile—a look of embarrassment.

Once in the car, Bell remained silent, unsure what to say. His head dropped down as if he was trying to hide his face. Morgan was also trying to figure out what to say. Every few minutes, Morgan would glance over in Bell's direction. If their eyes caught each other, they smiled. Having a conversation was difficult under the circumstances. Morgan finally turned and asked Bell why he was standing on a corner begging for money in Memphis.

"It's a long story," Bell replied.

"Tell me the story over lunch?"

Morgan pulled up to Davey's Diner, where locals would drop in during the wee hours or in the morning for an inexpensive full breakfast. It was mostly filled with workers, travelers, and retirees. There were several seniors and a few families with small children, but mostly laborers from the Department of Transportation. Morgan didn't know anyone because it was not his stomping ground, but he had heard great things about it.

The place had that diner look, a counter with stools, booths at the window to the left and the right, and more tables and chairs scattered in an open area. There were old photos of the owner with various patrons on the walls. The waitress was in her 50's, probably a grandmother, a little plump, and her hair tied back. She looked like she came with the place. The cook had an arm full of tattoos, a scruffy beard, and hair pulled into a bun. There was a group of retired-looking men off to one side. Morgan thought that could be him in fifty years.

"Sit wherever," yelled the owner.

He was in charge based on his demeanor and the photos on the wall. Morgan and Bell grabbed a booth. They sat and looked at each other, not saying a word. Morgan, again, broke the ice.

"So, what's up? I'm surprised to see you. Why are you in Memphis?"

"Mo," Bell said while shaking his head. "It's been real."

After Temple, he said he came home depressed about his

season-ending injury and unable to play ball. After surgery, there were months of recuperation, and it was clear he would not be the same athletically. Unfortunately, but not surprisingly, the school had moved on to other players. His injury was so bad that he would never be able to play again. The scholarship was gone, and he could not afford tuition without it.

Bell finally got a job as a truck driver and drove nationwide, delivering all kinds of goods. Mo remembered that Bell's older brother was a truck driver. That's how Bell got the gig. Driving a truck kept him busy and away from home, which is what he wanted. About two weeks ago, the job brought him to Memphis. It was the last stop of a long haul. When the truck emptied, they served termination papers without notice. Bell did not tell Mo the whole truth. The company was suspicious of him stealing a few things from the delivery. The orders were coming up short. When the problem was brought to the company's attention, the truck company had moved on, and there was no systematic method for checking the content. All they could surmise was that the driver was involved. It was their practice to terminate the employee immediately.

"I stayed in Memphis because I had nothing to return home to and didn't want anyone to know. My family already had these fantasies that I would be rich from playing in the pros. It was as if they were all depending on me. My girlfriend at Temple had already dumped me. That turned into a mess…"

Morgan looked at him, finding it hard to believe that Bell was in this situation. Unfortunately, shit happens, and he felt terrible for him.

"None of us are immune to bad things," Bell continued. "I haven't found work yet, so I move from shelter to shelter, when possible, to stay off the streets at night. These places give at least one meal daily."

Bell commented that he still has a big appetite and has to eat. They both laughed. Morgan was ready to get some food and hear more of the story. Bell did not ask Morgan why he was in Memphis or what he was doing. The waitress finally came over with a pot of coffee and two mugs and dropped off two menus.

Morgan shared his story about leaving home after high school and moving there to live with his aunt and uncle. He told Bell that he had an appointment at two o'clock for an apartment.

Morgan noticed Bell's face and hands.

"What happened? Your hands and face are all scarred and bloody. Looks like you were in a fight. Are you living mostly on the street?"

Bell reluctantly shared his story.

"After hours of panhandling on different street corners, I had accumulated a few dollars—just enough to buy something to eat. A few people drove by who were generous and gracious enough to give a helping hand. Of course, this isn't where I want to be, but that's the life I'm living for the moment. When evening came, I searched for a place to curl up, get out of the public eye, and sleep. Before I decided to crash there for the night, I looked around and thought it looked pretty safe. There was a slight breeze in the air. Everything was calm, quiet, and motionless. Eventually, I fell asleep.

"But around 1:00 AM, I was startled awake. Still on the

ground, I realized that out of nowhere, two guys were beating me up!"

"That's terrible," said Morgan.

"Yep, I guess it's something I never thought about."

Bell went on to tell him the guys were there to attack anyone they could find sleeping under the 5th Avenue Bridge, a known location for people experiencing homelessness. Police sometimes checked on the area. But that night, they were nowhere to be seen. There had been previous reports of individuals found dead or in terrible health condition at the location, but Bell didn't know any of that. All he knew was that he was getting his ass kicked.

He fought back as much as he could. As it turned out, the two perpetrators picked the wrong guy to mess with. They had no way of knowing his size and strength when he was on the ground asleep. They kicked him in his side and head. He could only curl up and try to protect himself, especially in the chest and face area. The strangers took turns and mostly connected with his arms and legs. He thought he would jump up and teach them a lesson as soon as he had the chance. He had to hold on a little longer. Finally, they got exhausted so Bell could stand up and fight back. He charged them like an offensive lineman pushing them back. His old football skills were now handy.

Bell weighed about 275 and stood 6' 7". He was solid muscle when he played football. Regardless, he was much bigger and began throwing one blow after another, knocking them down to the ground. When one tried to get up, they would receive a hard blow to the head and body. One of them started to bleed from the mouth. The other had a gash over his eye. They kept trying to attack but now found themselves trying to defend themselves from what they thought was a helpless man. He kept pounding and beating when he could get on top of one of the men, rendering him almost unconscious.

He will definitely need medical attention after tonight, Bell thought.

That's when one partner grabbed the other guy out from under Bell's clutches, and they both ran away. As they ran in one direction, Bell grabbed his possessions and ran in the opposite direction. Nobody else seemed to be around to see what had happened. There was no one to lend a helping hand. Who could he tell? He was indecisive about reporting the situation to the police. Who would believe him? That would only lead to questions about his identity and why he was there. He was not ready to answer any of those questions.

Bell was confident he had injured one of the men. Maybe a broken jaw or nose. He wondered what he would report to the nurse if he went to the hospital. Would they contact the police? He thought the story the next day would read, *Two men were walking down the street near the 5th Avenue Bridge and were attacked by a homeless man.* Maybe, the men were attacked by a robber, so the police would not be looking for Bell. That report would not be the truth, yet more believable.

Starting tomorrow, he would be sure to find one of the shelters that logged in men off the street at night. That morning he'd checked for physical damage to his body from their kicks. Although he was sore and in pain in several spots, nothing was broken or bleeding. Bell had his personal belongings and the little bit of money he carried in his money pouch. There was no time to feel sorry for himself. Instead, he prayed for an angel and waited for an opportunity to be saved.

Bell was known for telling fantastic stories when they were teens. Morgan was curious to know if this one was true. There was a news report on the radio early this morning of two guys being jumped and beaten last night. Morgan was wondering if that was related to Bell's story. He dared not ask. Today was not the time to test whether his story was true. Morgan owed him a favor. Back in school, Bell came to Morgan's rescue when a couple of bullies were harassing him. Before then, they were in History class together, but not friends. They would give a nod of the head to acknowledge the other. But until that day, had not been friends. It was Morgan's time to repay the favor, especially now since they were both members of the Watchmen.

"How about dinner tonight?" Morgan asked. "Is 6 PM okay?"

"Sure," said Bell. "Probably better to meet at the same intersection." Bell didn't want Morgan to feel sympathy for him, but everybody needs help.

"Getting one's life in order is complicated," said Morgan. "We have not seen each other for years, so let's make the best of this time to get caught up on things."

They both knew what they wanted to order from the menu, so browsing through it was quick. They ordered hamburgers with fried onion, fries, coleslaw, and large colas, as expected. Not much had changed from their days in high school. The waitress thanked them and left to place the order.

Morgan blurted out that he could not imagine what being homeless was like. Then he realized he should not have said that.

"A person goes through the day not knowing how to get through to the end. Some assistance is provided at a social service center or church, but not much is stable."

Bell said he thought about getting another trucking job, but that's not settling down. He was always on the road, traveling from place to place, meeting other truck drivers at various rest stops. Like Morgan, he had no training or education to do anything. All he ever did was play sports, and he excelled at it. He wished someone had told him to think about the possibility of not making it in the pros and to have a backup plan.

Morgan understood that Black men and women disproportionately experience homelessness compared to white folks. The shelters favor women because they often have children and for their safety. That leaves the Black man on the streets where the police harass them. Helping Bell to get a permanent place to live and a job was critical. This was not any Black man, this was one of his best friends.

While they waited for the food, Morgan was thinking about the apartment and whether he should invite Bell to stay with him. But it would be better if he found someone to help with the rent. Without a job, there was not much Bell could do. The food came, and they proceeded to chow down seriously.

"Thanks for the meal, Mo," said Bell.

"Glad I could do this much," responded Mo. "I'm glad we connected."

When they finished eating, they both got up from the booth. Morgan left a couple of dollars on the table for the tip, then went to the cashier to pay the bill. Outside, Morgan offered to drop Bell off wherever he wanted, but Bell said he would be okay. They agreed to meet again at 6 PM at the exact location where Morgan picked Bell up.

The time he spent with Bell was totally unexpected and outside his plans for the day. He had yet to pack. Morgan still needed to pick up KeTani, go to the apartment leasing office by 2:00 PM, and then go shopping for some furnishings, assuming the appointment went well.

He could hardly wait to tell KeTani about Bell. Then his mind went back to thinking about her rejection of moving in with him. Morgan was unsure if she was mad at him for not asking before today or just not interested.

Morgan flipped back to thinking about Bell and trying to find a way to help him out. He was convinced that Bell would lend him a hand if the situation was reversed. What could he do? It was clear to Morgan that he and his friends could all have benefitted from a mentor. The Watchmen had no real role models, at least none they noticed or talked about. None of them had the kind of fathers that spent time providing advice and guidance. The fathers all worked hard, and the mothers raised them. Tyler might have had guidance from a school counselor.

The Watchmen had each other, and that's all they needed at the time and that's all they wanted. It's now clear that they needed something more. Of the old gang, two are in prison, one is dead through his military service to this country, two are doing well with furthering their education, leaving Bell and Morgan who were trying to get their shit together.

As Morgan continued to reflect on the status of his old friends, he found the differences fascinating. They grew up together, sharing similar experiences, but the outcomes were vastly different.

CHAPTER 9

The Apartment

All day long, the radio station pumped out good R&B music through the car's speakers. Morgan could understand why his aunt enjoyed the station. The lyrics were easy to understand, and the melodies were fun to test your voice.

It was time for Morgan to pick up KeTani at work and head to the apartment leasing office. Following his conversation earlier in the day, he was uncertain about how she felt toward him. It was even more questionable whether Morgan should bring up the topic of her moving in with him again. Better to give her some time as she'd suggested. He didn't want her to get more upset.

He pulled into the parking lot close to the hospital staff entrance. He waited and waited for KeTani to emerge. It seemed to take forever. Then he realized he had arrived early. After the appointment, he would bring her back to get her car so she could head home to her apartment. Grace Gardens, the relatively new apartments, were located in the Bourneside neighborhood, an older, very dense residential area. It had primarily single-family homes that lined the streets. Some of the newer homes were two-level homes, which retirees from the north wanted and could afford to build. The area felt peaceful and quiet, but occasionally, there were reports of petty crimes. In general, Morgan thought the area would be safe.

The usual commercial businesses were nearby, like a grocery store and a few restaurants for takeout or a casual breakfast, lunch, or dinner. There was an elementary school within walking distance, but he had no children to worry about, and a Methodist church was two blocks away. He had attended a Baptist church as a child but had not regularly attended church since he moved to Memphis, to the dismay of his family.

Morgan's parents regularly attended church. His father was a deacon, and his mother sang in the choir. She had a lovely voice, good enough to sing lead on a few of the choir selections. As a result of their involvement, Morgan regularly attended until he reached sixteen. That's when they allowed him to make his own decision. Some of his friends attended North United Methodist Church, so that's where he went on occasion. There was less shouting and dancing in the aisles, and he did not feel out of place if he did not wear a tie.

KeTani finally exited the building and jumped into the car.

"Hey, beautiful," said Mo. And she gave the usual reply. Morgan pulled off focused on their next stop—the new apartment.

"So, what kept you busy these past few hours?" KeTani asked.

Morgan was excited to tell her about Bell. He told her he was driving down the street and saw Bell standing on the corner.

"Who is Bell?"

Morgan described him as one of his closest friends from home.

"He's homeless?" asked KeTani.

"Yes, but there's a reason. We went to Davey's for lunch and he told me the backstory."

Morgan shared Bell's story about how he ended up here after getting fired. He did not want to tell her all of Bell's story because it wasn't really his story to tell.

"Wow, that sounds crazy," KeTani acknowledged.

"Yes, it was totally unexpected," said Mo. "Neither of us knew the other was here."

He told her it was the first time they had talked since leaving high school. Bell had not been in touch with any of the other Watchmen after he left for college to play football. Morgan told her about the shelters being hit or miss and that he was considering inviting Bell to be his roommate. KeTani was surprised at the possibility and asked if he no longer wanted her to move in.

"No, that's not it," Mo stated emphatically.

He wanted to be with her, but he needed a backup plan if she said no. Damn, he was trying not to bring up the topic. They sat in silence for the rest of the drive to the apartment.

They finally arrived at Grace Gardens with ten minutes to spare. They looked around the grounds, and liked what they saw. The lawn was nicely mowed, shrubs trimmed, and no trash was in sight. There were a few cars in the parking spaces. There was no pool or garages. The Commons was the building where the management office was situated and with some community rooms for social gatherings. The mailboxes for each unit were there, in addition, several bookcases filled with books, DVDs, and games.

Ms. Latham could be spotted in the office with an attractive couple. The man and woman looked like they were slightly older, professional types. He wore a suit and tie as if he had come from work. They appeared to be wrapping up, so Morgan and KeTani sat on the couch to wait their turn. Morgan was pleased that she was there. KeTani could see the place for herself, give her approval, and ask the questions he would not know to ask. Ms. Latham appeared much younger than Morgan thought she would be, probably a little older than himself. She was dressed in slacks and a striped blouse. She wore a necklace and earrings but no other jewelry. Her hair was natural in braids that were professionally styled. Ms. Latham was all about business.

Until now, he only talked with her on the phone or via email. He did not expect her to be Black. Usually, you can tell by the voice on the phone, but he was wrong this time.

She approached them and asked, "Are you Morgan?"

"Yes, ma'am."

She stuck out her hand and said, "Call me June."

"This is my friend KeTani." Mo was polite and cordial.

They both said hello. June offered to give them a tour of the apartment. She asked if they were looking for a one-bedroom or a two-bedroom.

"Both, if that's okay," Morgan answered.

"Let me get the keys," said Ms. Latham.

With the keys in hand, they walked out of the building, across the complex, and entered Building C. June then began her spiel.

"The one-bedroom comes with one parking space, and the two-bedroom has two spaces. There is at least one unassigned parking space per apartment for guests throughout the complex."

They entered a one-bedroom, which was perfect for Morgan and might work for them if KeTani decided to move in. The two-bedroom would be more than his budget, but if Morgan shared the apartment with anyone else, he would need a two-bedroom. Overall, the apartments were nicely designed with great square footage. All apartment unit came with electric heat included in the rental fee.

The apartments look so different when empty compared to the lovely photos in the brochure. On the website, they were nicely furnished. Morgan wanted to believe the apartments came furnished like that when rented. He was beginning to imagine what furnishings he would minimally need to buy for the place to feel like a home. A place to sit, a TV set, and a way to play music. A table and chairs for eating a meal, a bedroom set, and lamps. Not to mention, he did not have any kitchenware. Morgan had nothing.

They returned to the office and sat across from June at her desk. She pulled out Morgan's application to review the information. According to his form, Morgan was living with family members. She asked questions to verify what she had read. He acknowledged that they were his aunt and uncle.

"Your employer?"

"City Medical Center," replied Morgan. "KeTani works there too. That's where we met," he responded.

KeTani whispered to Morgan that he was giving more information than needed. What June needed to know was if the apartment would be for one or both. They had not made that decision yet. The rent was $950 for the one-bedroom and $1,200 for the two-bedroom. Ms. June stated she needed a one-month deposit and the first month's rent.

"Which type of apartment do you wish to leave a deposit on?" asked June.

"A one-bedroom." Morgan reached into his pocket and handed Ms. June the bank check for the total amount.

"KeTani, if you decide to move into the apartment, you will need to fill out a form, too, so we can get all your personal information as a resident. Morgan, give me a moment to prepare your lease agreement."

KeTani looked at Morgan sternly. She wanted to discuss the matter after they left. It's a good thing that Morgan had been saving his money. Although the rent sounded tight, living in his apartment was worth the sacrifice. It would be much better if he could convince KeTani to move in.

Morgan and KeTani stepped out of the office and back into the common area. That's when Morgan noticed the bulletin board with a job listing for a maintenance man at Grace Gardens. Morgan stuck his head back into the office.

"Ms. June, is that job, the maintenance position, still open?"

"Yes, why?"

"This is for a friend. He just moved here from my hometown and needs to find work and a place to stay. I can bring him here tomorrow. What does it pay, and are there any benefits?"

"The pay is minimum, but the benefit is the person gets to live here at no cost."

"That sounds great for him right now. His name is Bell. Thanks. What would be a good time for you to meet him?"

"How does 10:30 AM work?"

"We'll be here."

Ms. Latham finished preparing the lease agreement and had Morgan sign it. She then handed him the keys.

"Welcome! I'm sure you will love it here. There are a lot of residents around your age. I'm sure you will get to know them."

As they exited The Commons, three young ladies were walking by. They were all attractive, dressed like they were getting ready to step out for the night. Each offered a friendly greeting, and Morgan and KeTani did the same. One of them asked if he was moving in. Mo was quick to reply, yes. KeTani said nothing. The girls wanted him to know they were available to help him if he needed anything. They lived in Building C, unit 22. Morgan was up one flight in unit 33. One of the young ladies observed that KeTani was not saying a word.

"Are you moving here too?" One of them asked.

KeTani glared at her and said, "Thinking about it."

"Okay."

They all looked at Morgan and said, "Stop by anytime."

KeTani looked at Morgan as if to say, *oh no, you won't.* Now she had to think fast about leaving her man in the clutches of these fast women. She trusted Morgan, but she did not know them. KeTani understood women like them. They flirt, tease, and would try to steal her man. She and Morgan got into the car. He was smiling because he was getting his apartment. KeTani's mind was still focused on those ladies, and she wondered why Morgan was smiling.

"Morgan, I don't want to see you hanging around those

ladies when I come to see you," she said abruptly.

"Of course not beautiful, but it would help if you were around a lot, so they don't get the wrong idea."

Within a few minutes, they agreed to wait until the next day to shop for furniture. It was too late in the day to begin, plus Morgan had dinner plans with Bell. They would start by making a list of stuff to purchase and try to arrange for delivery where possible. Morgan let KeTani know profusely that he wanted help.

Now that she has seen the place, she may be interested in moving. He could tell that she liked it a lot. She indicated she still needed more time to consider moving in and expressed how hard a decision was for her. There was a lot for her to consider. She now had to factor these ladies into her decision. She hadn't thought about anything like this before. KeTani had to decide how much she liked or loved Morgan and whether living together made it better or worse.

Morgan could hardly wait to let Bell know that he had recommended him for a job opportunity that would also mean housing and him no longer living on the street.

Morgan returned to the hospital where he and KeTani discussed the various stores they would shop for items and what he might need.

Morgan said to KeTani, "Take whatever time is necessary to decide about moving. Being together is the most important thing to me. I'm hoping you want the same."

"Morgan, I like you a lot. That's not the issue. But I had not planned to change apartments. I want us to be together, but not like a married couple that's not married. I don't want to start a family and put aside all my dreams. More importantly, it would be best if you didn't move forward without me," said KeTani. "I will try to make a decision very soon. Talk to you later tonight."

CHAPTER 10

To Pack or Not

Morgan lost valuable time after stopping by the hospital, the bank, and sitting down with Bell, to have a bite to eat. By early evening, he was supposed to be packed and be ready to move. That did not happen.

He returned home. The house was empty, as expected. His room was in the usual state of disarray. He would try to tidy it sometimes but that was not his habit. Clothes would be thrown over a chair or sometimes on the floor, whether clean or dirty. They were never in a big pile, but just enough stuff so it required some attention. Morgan rarely made his bed. He would throw the covers back to make it look neat but not take the time to tuck it all in at the corners. His parents tried to get him to neatly make up his bed every morning, but he never developed the habit.

Then there were the papers of all kinds. Morgan was never taught how to organize his information in a filing system. His mail, the bills he had to pay, newspapers, magazines, and books were everywhere: piles of paper of all types. He had difficulty sorting items to keep and other items to throw away.

For Morgan, packing his belongings was more about

cleaning his bedroom, so for the next hour, he did that. He threw away papers, made his bed, picked up the clothes, and separated the clean from the dirty. The dirty clothes went into the laundry basket, and the clean ones were folded neatly and placed in one of the suitcases. Morgan had a few books, mostly related to his job, that he had to read when studying for certification. They got placed in a box along with a few other personal items.

He stopped to take a brief break and started to think about what was ahead—the morning got off to a good start and then got off track. It took a while to get his check, but he got it. The biggest surprise was seeing Bell. His biggest disappointment was KeTani's indecision about moving into the apartment. He then remembered the black zipper-locked pouch he received from Aunt Mae in the morning. What was in it? How was he to figure out how to unlock it? There was no key. He was without a hint of the three-numbered combination. The cloth material was too thick to cut open. Opening the pouch needed to remain a secret a little longer. It had already been four years. How bad could another day or two be? He threw it back on his dresser to fight with the pouch later.

Having an apartment, a place he could call his own was finally being accomplished. Not having parents or relatives tell him what to do would be great. It took forever to reach this point, and it finally arrived. The longer he thought about the reality of making this move, the more insecure he got. Morgan did not know how to cook, nor was he fully aware of all the responsibilities he would now have. None of his family ever sat with him to educate him about renting an apartment. All he knew was that other people his age did it, so why not him?

Morgan worked a well-paying job and had been able to save his money. He did not know how much he might need and what the total cost might be. That's one of the reasons, besides his love for her, he wanted KeTani to move in. She had the experience of living in an apartment. Morgan was "way out on a limb," and the weight of it all might break unless he found more support. He now wished he had talked to his uncle and aunt more. Morgan did not want them to say, *It's okay for you to stay here with us.* He rejected talking with his parents, despite knowing they would help. Morgan wanted to do things on his terms and surprise them. He will soon be able to announce this to them and everyone else.

Did he want Bell, or anyone, as a roommate other than KeTani? Morgan had not seen Bell in years. He might not be the same person he knew in high school. But his offer to him was not as a permanent roommate, but temporary arrangement until Bell could get on his feet. Morgan believed Bell would have done the same for him if it were reversed. This was his homeboy, and he needed help.

Just then, Morgan came across a box in the closet. He had forgotten it was there. It contained a pile of old photos and other stuff. The photos were mostly of him but also his mom and dad. His mom was correct when she mentioned he rarely called home. He did miss his parents a hell of a lot. They always showed how much they loved him and always wanted the best for him. However, Morgan got tired of the questions. Regardless, he missed his parents. He missed being home and hanging out with friends.

Most boys have dreams about making it huge in this world. Aside from hitting the lottery for millions, they think about material things requiring a highly paid job. It did not matter what career he selected as long as it provided more than sufficient income to afford everything he desired. Owning a mansion, or driving a nice foreign car, like a Mercedes or Lamborghini, would be nice but Morgan did not need those things to define him.

He needed to figure out who he wanted to be without attending college or entering the armed forces. The best thing would be to start a business, he thought. Be the boss. You decide how many hours to work, when, and how. The staff will follow your lead. Morgan did not have the skills to be a plumber or electrician. He was not interested in operating a funeral home and having to see dead bodies every day. He did not have the creative talent of an artist or musician. All he had to do was figure out what interested him enough to learn about it and offer it to whoever would buy it. He wondered if he should find a sales job at a large company with offices nationwide and work his way up the ladder.

His current job provided some possibilities. Medical centers need people who do all types of things. It's like a small city unto itself. He learned that he is comfortable around people. He liked the hustle and busy atmosphere. Within the center's structure, you can get trained on anything that requires certification or administers a support service. Helping a doctor was exciting, knowing that you were part of a team that treated a patient. Morgan believed he was in the right place to find an opportunity he could never imagine.

Morgan looked at his watch and started heading to where he would pick up Bell. He could hardly wait to hear more about what he had been doing.

Dinner

Bell arrived early for the pickup. He spotted a man holding a sign on the corner where he had stood earlier in the day. That's where Morgan would be looking. Bell approached the man and told him he needed to find another corner. They didn't argue about the location at first. Neither owned it, but to Bell, this guy was new and encroaching on the intersection he had carved out the past few days.

They went back and forth, neither wanting to give in to the other. Their volume was kept low so no one nearby could hear them talking. Bell knew he was not staying for long, but it was the principle of the matter. Bell had enough, so he pushed the guy to ensure he understood he would fight him for the spot. Bell usually had a mild temper. His friends thought of him as a big teddy bear. However, if you watched him play football, you would notice he can be challenging.

Finally, the other guy gave up and decided to find somewhere else. Besides, Bell was twice his size, and to pick a fight would be insane. They both turned and took a few steps off the curb and into the street. Suddenly, a car came out of nowhere and hit the man, throwing him in the air about ten feet. You could hear the tires screeching to a halt and the thump of the impact. The driver was startled momentarily. He looked around quickly and then sped off down the street. Several people nearby came over to help the man lying in the street. Bell wondered if the man was still alive.

Morgan was en route to pick up Bell for dinner. Gladys Knight was finishing up on the radio, and then one of his favorites came on, Marvin Gaye's *"What's Going On?"* The song was interrupted by a news story.

Breaking news! A major traffic jam is at the intersection of Main and 5th Street. We are unclear about the cause or how long this tie-up will last. We're working on getting these details. Try to avoid this area. Use either of the parallel streets as an alternative.

In other news, the police are still investigating the beating incident from last night. They have a description but no suspect.

That's the location for picking up Bell. Morgan kept driving, and traffic moved slower as he got closer. He turned his head from side to side, hoping to find Bell standing on one of the other corners. Police lights flashed from every direction. Morgan counted seven police cars, an ambulance, and a fire truck. The police were trying to wave the onlookers forward. He could not see Bell, and there was no way to know if that was him in the ambulance. Morgan couldn't pull over to park the car, so he took his time driving through the intersection.

He was beginning to imagine something tragic might have happened. So many police and emergency vehicles must mean somebody was hurt or all bloodied up. Morgan's mind was processing the worst-case scenario, although he had never seen a dead person or anyone severely injured. What would he do if it was Bell? Would he need to reach his parents, who may not know he lived in this city?

He heard a few loud knocks—boom, boom, boom, on the car window. Morgan reacted as he got through the tie-up. It scared him at first. He looked to his left side, and there was Bell. Morgan was so relieved to see him. Morgan motioned for him to get in the car.

"Did you see what happened? Were you here when it happened? I was worried it was you!" Morgan yelled.

Bell looked as if nothing had happened. He was either in shock or disbelief. Just like before, he was silent, not saying a word. Bell started to process what just happened.

After he heard the noise, he kept walking to cross the busy street and did not look back. He moved to blend into the small crowd, pretending to be an onlooker so he could slip away. He didn't want anyone to associate him with the incident. He was not sure if he would be blamed. He explained to Morgan that he and a guy were talking. As they parted ways, the man stepped into the street and was hit by a car. The car sped off, leaving the young man lying in the street. Bell described the man as looking about their age, between twenty and twenty-five years old. The ambulance and the police arrived on the scene within minutes. He was another homeless man.

There was the attack by two men last night, and now this. It seemed as though trouble will find you when you're the most vulnerable. It was not his fault. The guy did not look before moving forward. Regardless, Bell felt guilty because he asked the guy to move. The driver should have stayed to see if the man was injured, but instead, he left the scene. An awful hit and run.

"He must be dead after getting run over like that," Bell said. "I couldn't do anything to help him, and I have my own problems to deal with. I'm looking forward to dinner, Mo. I just want to forget this happened."

Bell did not utter another word about the incident. Morgan felt he would say something when he was ready. They drove off and headed to Sam's Seafood Shack, another favorite spot for eating out. They walked in and waited for the hostess to be seated. The place was packed with families having dinner and small groups of men and women drinking beer and giant margaritas at the bar. The smell of fried seafood was in the air, and the noise level was almost too high for conversation. Their seats were in clear view of the large TV with an NFL game broadcasting.

The waitress dropped the menus and asked to take their drink orders. It made Morgan realize that he and Bell had never been out drinking. The few times they had alcohol as high school students were at house parties but never legally at a bar or restaurant.

"What can I get you?"

Bell immediately said, "A beer, whatever is on tap."

"A small or pint size?" she asked.

"Pint," he replied.

Morgan wasn't yet sure what he wanted but he knew it was not a beer, especially that size.

"How about a rum and coke?"

She asked, "Is Bacardi okay?"

He replied, "Yes."

The waitress then asked to see their IDs. They proudly reached into their pockets, took out their wallets, and showed her their identification. She returned later with the drinks, they placed their food order, and they had time to talk.

Morgan looked at Bell and proceeded enthusiastically, telling him the good news about a possible job and a place for him to live.

Bell looked at him, slightly confused. He was shocked to hear that he might have a job and place to live and wanted to know the catch. It was too good to be true. Morgan repeated what he'd said to make sure it was clear and Bell wasn't still thinking about that man being hit by a car.

"There is a job opening for a maintenance man at the apartment building. The person would be on call for things in the evening and on weekends. The best part is that the job comes with a studio apartment with no rent fees." Morgan explained.

Morgan asked if Bell was interested and told him he already set up an appointment for 10:30 AM the next day.

Bell looked amazed and said, "I don't know anything about maintenance."

Morgan looked back at him and said, "How about a 'thank you' first? What does a maintenance man need to know? How to change a light bulb, clean up a mess, or call a plumber or an electrician."

Morgan believed this could change Bell's current situation immediately.

"How about it?" Morgan asked.

"Give me a minute," Bell replied. He then asked Mo, "Do you believe in God?"

Mo was unsure how to respond and what it had to do with the job, but he answered.

"I guess. Why?"

Bell explained. Last Sunday, he stopped by this church, unsure if he could recall the name. He approached the altar when the pastor invited members to do so. The minister asked them to bow their heads, reach out, and hold each other's hands. Bell said he prayed to God that he would send an angel.

Bell looked at Morgan and said, "I expected something in a spiritual form, not a human form."

While growing up, Bell did not attend church. None of his family were regular church members. He started going with some of the other football team members at Temple. One of the guys was a preacher's kid or PK, and was always talking about God in his life. The football players would always say a prayer at practices and games. And they went to church every Sunday if they weren't traveling.

"Today, you and I find each other after years of being disconnected. Neither one of us was looking for the other. It just happened. Was that a coincidence, a concurrence of circumstances, that brought us together again, or was this predetermined, a kind of divine intervention?"

"Later, on the same day, a person was involved in a hit and run by standing on the same corner where I stood earlier today."

Bell wondered if that was supposed to be him, but not because he was waiting to be picked up, so the next poor soul who stood in that spot lost their life. Or better yet, was he the lucky one? No matter what you believe, he avoided being hit.

"You are telling me about a job and a place to live. I need both of these things but had not asked you for either. Is this a gift from God or just my lucky day? Have my prayers been answered?"

Morgan looked bewildered, trying to understand how Bell assessed what was happening to him. And only Bell could answer that question. Morgan had not pondered his faith and belief in God before. He would always identify himself as a Christian despite not attending church. At home, they always blessed their food before eating. But he was not an active church member and never thought about how God provides. The preacher says, *"He steps right in on time when you need him."*

Most of the time, Morgan would think about things happening by chance or because of his efforts. He had no way of explaining why and how they met today. But if they had not, he would not have paid attention to the job notice in the apartment leasing office and would not have been at Davey's Diner early today nor sitting there right now. Because they reconnected, his day changed. He believed it was for the betterment of both of them. Is it God, chance, luck, or coincidence? He couldn't say.

For the next hour, Morgan and Bell spent time reminiscing about their many adventures during high school. They recalled running away from a corner convenience store one night after one of the guys stole some candy bars. It was so easy back then to steal candy that sat out on the rack. They ran hard through an unfamiliar neighborhood until they came upon a wired fence. Everyone got over okay except Morgan, who got his pants leg caught on the fence, attempting to climb over. They chuckled at the sight of his torn pants.

"We were all scared we would get caught. You were mostly scared of your parents when they saw your pants," remembered Bell. "Okay. Let's go check out this job and the apartment," Bell said.

They had finished their fish and chip dinners and were looking at the list of desserts.

The conversation was interrupted by Morgan's phone ringing. It was Aunt Mae.

"Hey, what's up?" He didn't realize who he was speaking to and quickly changed his speech to, "Hi, Aunt Mae. This is Morgan."

"Morgan, come pick me up!" she screamed. "Tre was taken to the medical center earlier today. He was working a double shift and collapsed. He works so hard and needs to slow down. Can you get here soon?"

"Yes, right away. My friend Bell is with me. Is it okay if he comes along?"

"Who is Bell?" she asked, "and where did he come from?"

"He's from back home. We were close friends in high school."

"Okay, then of course. Right now, please just come pick me up from the house.

"Yes, Aunt Mae," he politely answered.

CHAPTER 12

Uncle T

They left the restaurant and drove as quickly as they could to pick up Aunt Mae. She would be waiting at the front door, probably pacing until he arrived. Generally, she was patient, but this was not the moment. Morgan relayed to Bell what Aunt Mae had told him. He was not sure what the problem was or how serious. But Aunt Mae sounded frantic.

"Come along for the ride. Aunt Mae was okay with you being there."

Morgan thought, *what if he had a heart attack or stroke?* Uncle T was so strong-headed that he would wake up and try to go to work. It's hard to keep a good man like that down. He needed to ensure Aunt Mae got to the hospital and talked to him. She's the only person he would listen to.

He pulled up in front of the house. Aunt Mae walked quickly towards the car. Bell got out, opened the door for her, and said, "Hello, ma'am. I'm Bell."

He hopped into the back seat. She did not respond. Aunt Mae was not trying to be impolite, she just had more on her mind. She finally turned around in her seat.

"Hello, young man," to return the greeting. "Thank you for opening the car door. It's nice to meet a young man with manners."

Aunt Mae turned to Mo and started talking about her husband. She tried to get him to eat better. Aunt Mae described his behavior and habits.

"He never eats enough fruits and vegetables. Plus, he has an alcoholic drink every night. He doesn't need that stuff. He only gets exercise when he mows the lawn or rakes the leaves. Tre works those long hours and tried to do a double shift today. He's always worried about not having enough money to pay the bills. He is almost at retirement age, but I doubt he would if given a chance. He may not make it if he keeps going the way he does. Lord knows he needs to slow down and take better care of himself."

"Do you know what happened, Aunt Mae?" asked Mo.

"No, not really. They say he just fainted."

"The people at his work called 911 for help, and the medics put him on a stretcher and took him to the Emergency Room where you work, Mo. The office tried to reach me, but I didn't hear the phone ring."

Later the hospital called and told her where he was. She did not believe it was life-threatening.

"Baby, I'm sorry," she said.

"For what?" Mo asked.

"How did it go at the apartment?"

"Great. I got the place but didn't have time to purchase furniture or household items or finish packing. I'll probably need a few days to a week."

She was happy for him and made sure he knew there was

no rush to move out.

Aunt Mae asked Bell where he was living.

Morgan jumped in and explained, "He just arrived in the city and needed a permanent place to stay."

"Well, honey, stay with us for a while. If you're a friend of Mo, then you're a friend of the family."

Mo jumped in to speak again. "He has an interview in the morning that provides a place to live."

"That's good, but until then, you're staying with us."

Despite all the stress, Aunt Mae had time to be generous.

Bell looked at Morgan and said, "I told you God had given me an angel."

They arrived at the hospital. Mo pulled up to the entrance so Aunt Mae could go inside. Morgan drove to the visitor's lot to park. They ran from the car to catch up to Aunt Mae.

The receptionist said, "Mr. Jackson was brought to Section D on the 4th floor. The nurse's station there will be able to help you."

After speaking with the head nurse, they were told he was in Room 449.

"Is he talking enough for us to visit with him?" Aunt Mae asked.

"Yes."

Bell was not family, so he went down the hall to a waiting area. Uncle T. was lying up in bed, half asleep. Aunt Mae reached over to touch him.

"How are you feeling?"

He nodded to acknowledge he was better, considering he was connected to a bunch of tubes and wires. He had an oxygen mask on, an IV connection in his left arm, and something else connected to his right. There were connections all over his chest to monitor his heartbeat.

"What are they telling you, Tre?"

He began moving around so he could arouse himself from sleep and could talk.

He could not speak clearly, "They ran some tests in ER and again when I got settled into this room. My blood pressure is up, and my sugar is elevated. They plan to keep me overnight. Not sure if it was a mild stroke or just exhaustion and dehydration," muttered Tre.

He described what happened. He got dizzy, felt his legs give out from under him, and passed out at work. He was unsure how long he was on the floor. Fortunately, a few other workers were around him. When he woke up, the medics were there. His speech sounded slurred, but he had no injuries from falling.

Aunt Mae stood there, not knowing what to say or do next. It was obvious that Uncle T needed to rest, and her being there asking him questions was not helping. She wanted to stay in the room watching over her man until she could talk with the doctor to get more information. They had planned to monitor him overnight and check his vitals in the morning. The usual procedures called for more tests to determine if things was more serious or if he could be released to rest at home.

Morgan did not know the medical staff in that unit. He spent more time in the area where patients were recovering after surgery. He returned to the desk and introduced himself so the on-duty nurses would know he worked at the medical center.

"Hello, again. Let me introduce myself."

"Okay," she said, but it looked like she had heard this act from family members who thought it would result in better care.

"My name is Morgan. My friends call me Mo. I work here at City Medical Center." He produced his badge to verify what he was saying. The nurse looked up and smiled.

She replied, "It's nice to meet you," with a slightly better attitude. "My name is Samantha, but everyone calls me Sam."

Before he could say more, she assured him they would keep a close eye overnight and attend to his uncle's needs.

"He's in good hands. Trust me." Morgan acknowledged her with a nod and was satisfied.

With nothing more he could do at the nurse's station, he went to the waiting area where Bell was watching the football game. He was anxious to see the end of the game.

Bell asked, "How's your uncle?"

"Resting," Morgan answered.

"Do they know what's wrong yet?"

"No, Aunt Mae is waiting to talk with a doctor."

That's when his phone rang. It was KeTani. Morgan told her what was happening and that he would love to talk with her after returning home. She understood. She asked if she could do anything.

"Just be awake when I call late tonight."

It was comforting to hear her voice. He wanted to talk then, but not with Bell sitting there beside him. Once they got home and could relax, he would call her back.

Within a few minutes after hanging up, the phone rang again. This time it was his dad.

"Hi, Dad," Morgan said.

"Hey, son, how are you?"

"I'm okay, but Uncle T is in the hospital."

He said he already knew. "Aunt Mae called and your mom

asked me to call you. Is Tre okay?"

Morgan said he was unsure what was happening but was waiting at the hospital to find out.

He informed his dad that he had got the apartment. His dad offered a few words of encouragement.

"This is an important step you're making, but I'm sure you prepared yourself for whatever comes your way."

Morgan said he needed to hear that from him. He described the place to his dad, so he would not think it was some run-down room on the wrong side of town.

Then Morgan said, "You won't believe it. Bell is here. Remember him from my high school?"

"Yeah, of course. What's he doing there?"

"Didn't he get injured playing football, dropped out, and returned home?"

"It's a long story," Morgan replied. "Better to share another day rather than over the phone."

His father then apologized to him. Louis recognized that he had been tough on Mo through high school. He could not understand what was happening in his head concerning his future. He was sorry if he pushed too hard and forced Mo to leave home. In the end, he believed Mo made an excellent decision to still be around family, find a place where he could take the time to figure it out, and be able to move forward. He realized that Morgan needed time and space, a lot more than he was willing to provide.

"As your parents, we are here to help you continue your journey on whatever path you take."

Morgan was stunned and unable to react. He had never heard his father sound so encouraging.

"Son, Mom and I will be flying in to see Aunt Mae and you tomorrow. You know your mom. She wants to be there to help her sister. This will give us some time for me to hear about all the things you're doing."

"You're coming here to visit? That's great," Morgan responded.

"We also want to help you move into your new place and, if necessary, purchase the furniture you might need. You can't do this alone, son. We all need some help along the way. Let us help."

"Yes, sir. I hear you, and if I'm being honest, I could use some help."

After he finished the call, Morgan looked up at Bell.

"I guess you can tell that was my parents. They're coming tomorrow. The house will be packed with all of us."

Bell was more focused on the game than Morgan's phone conversations. Bell was happy to be off the streets. He was thrilled to have a place to stay and was not worried about finding shelter tonight. He had two great meals today courtesy of his good friend Mo.

"I'm going back to see how Aunt Mae is doing. I'll be back," said Morgan.

By now, Morgan hoped the doctor on duty had stopped by to provide information on Uncle T's situation. He expected things to be okay since there was no blood or broken bones, and he was conscious and able to speak. Hospitals like to keep you overnight for observations so they won't face any repercussions for releasing you too early.

Then it all happened in the blink of an eye. Three police officers came to the floor looking for a possible suspect.

CHAPTER 13

The Cops

The police noticed Bell sitting in the waiting area. Once he was spotted, they started yelling commands without asking questions. The cops had a basic description of the suspect, Black, about 6' 2" tall, wearing a hoodie, but not the name of someone they were searching for. Bell was startled immediately and did as they demanded. One police officer told him to get on his knees. Another shouted, "Put your hands in the air!" There were three of them in uniform with a look of determination. He was lucky they were not excessively brutal without cause, but it was a scary moment.

Bell had never felt fearful. But the police always stressed him out. He froze in place, trying desperately not to cause them to use excessive force. As a Black kid in the city, you believe it's them against us. Tonight was not the time to test his rights against law enforcement. Bell was thinking about all the bad things he had done since arriving in the city and which one he could be arrested for. Were they finally picking him up for the two men he beat down in the middle of the night? Or was it for the snacks he stole at the convenience store? Ultimately, it didn't matter. He would prefer not to go to jail.

The police reached for a pair of handcuffs. It was a case of acting now and asking questions later. By the time they brought him to the police station, they would be convinced he was the suspect. Morgan, however, was not sure why Bell was being singled out. It might have been related to the two men who were beaten.

Morgan was hesitant to step in. He did not want to become the center of the police officer's rage by asking questions that made them uncomfortable. But how could he not speak to protect his brother?

Finally, Morgan spoke up.

"What is this about? I work here at the medical center. Who are you looking for? This man has been with me most of the day, and we are here now with my aunt looking in on my uncle. Why are you arresting him?"

The cops looked at Morgan as if to ask why he was interrupting them.

"Stand back and stay out of this!" shouted one of the officers. "If you don't, you can be arrested for interfering."

Morgan wondered if it had something to do with the car crash earlier that evening. Was Bell possibly involved in some manner? There was no indication of any involvement. If he was involved, he indeed kept it to himself. Did he walk away from an incident where someone was hurt or died? When I scooped him from the street corner, it appeared he had nothing to do with anything related to the accident. Would Morgan be wrapped up in this thing as well if he had? He wondered.

The police officers noticed the crowd of people watching the confrontation unfold.

One of the officers said, "This man is a possible suspect in a robbery about two hours ago. The suspect might have been injured, so we're checking the medical center to see if anyone came here looking to be treated. We were told he might be here."

"I can assure you that he was with me at Sam's Seafood Shack. Here is the receipt," Morgan interjected. "After we left there, we drove to this address. He showed him his driver's license. This is where I live with my uncle and aunt. This man," Morgan purposely did not say Bell's name, "is from my hometown and is staying with us. This must be a mistake." Morgan stated. "He's not here for medical treatment."

Bell kept absolutely quiet and physically still so as not to provoke a response from the police. Morgan was pleasantly surprised by Bell's calm behavior. He did not try to speak, move, resist, or do anything that could be misconstrued. He left the talking up to Morgan. Fortunately, a small crowd was watching. Some knew Morgan worked there and could back him up if necessary. The officers looked around to see if anyone was using a phone to capture the incident on video. They did not want to be featured in a nightly news report. After one of the cops looked at the receipt Morgan handed him, he signaled to his partner to stand down.

"This does not prove anything about this man," the officer said.

He then reached up to touch his earpiece to receive a message. Morgan told the officers they were at the hospital because his aunt had to see her husband. He was not there to be treated as you described and has been in the waiting room watching the football game. After a few minutes, the police officer released Bell and treated the incident as a mistaken identity but offered no apology. None whatsoever.

"The suspect is in police custody."

Aunt Mae had made her way down the hall to see what had happened and noticed Morgan in the middle of it all. As if this commotion did not matter.

She said, "It's time to go."

Morgan looked at the police, and they were satisfied. Bell was released and moved next to his friend Morgan to get the hell out of there.

She had talked to the doctor and must wait until morning for an update. Morgan told her he had spoken with his dad, and they were arriving tomorrow. He was ready to go. Aunt Mae asked Morgan what the cops wanted. Morgan told her they were about to arrest Bell, but soon after, they realized they had the wrong person.

The cops left the floor. The small crowd began to move on with what each person was doing. The nurses and doctors turned their attention back to their patients. Morgan stopped by to see Uncle T before leaving.

"See you tomorrow. Get lots of rest," Morgan said."

He turned and glanced at Aunt Mae to see if he could sense the seriousness of the situation.

Morgan looked at Bell. He seemed to be in shock. He looked as if he had no idea where or why he was there. The incident with the cops was probably more than he could handle.

"You okay?" asked Morgan.

"Not really."

"Do you want to talk about it?"

"Maybe later or tomorrow."

Bell told him he had stolen some items from a convenience store a few days ago. He was hungry and needed something to eat. It wasn't much, just some chips and beef jerky. He thought it had something to do with that.

"You know how we used to do as kids," said Bell.

He didn't think much of it. Stealing candy, chips, or cookies was easy. They'd have five or six guys spread out across the store, because the clerk could not keep an eye on everyone. Thank goodness it was another person they were looking for this time, not him.

"Thanks for your help, Mo." He was unsure what would have happened had Mo not been there.

Bell had never been approached by the police like that before. In news stories, sometimes the alleged suspect looks like the victim, all beaten and bloody. He did not want to look like that, especially for a few snacks. It's so common to get pulled over for speeding or DWB (driving while Black). They check your license and registration while you sit and hope that's all. But three cops looking for someone is frightening.

"I almost pissed in my pants. That was no joke," Bell added.

It would be better if Morgan did not know the truth about the attack from the two men as well as his involvement with the guy on the street corner. Both of those were more serious than stealing.

They went back downstairs, out the hospital exit, and drove off as quickly as possible. Morgan had seen enough of the medical center for one day. Aunt Mae told Morgan that they needed to go by where Uncle T worked to pick up his car.

"You know how he is about his car. He would not want it

sitting in that parking lot overnight for someone to mess with it. Mo, you can drive his car, and I will take mine, and we will meet at home. There is some sweet potato pie waiting for us."

She baked it, especially for Morgan, to celebrate getting the apartment.

Aunt Mae looked at Bell and said, "Things will feel better once we get home and relax. You will need to forget about it, young man."

CHAPTER 14

End of the Day

Finally, at about 11:00 PM, they headed home. Aunt Mae drove her car. They stopped by the place where Uncle T worked. His car was parked in a safe place to prevent another driver from scratching it with their door. He was very particular about where he parked, not trusting anyone to be careful not to hit his pride and joy. He never parked under a tree to avoid tree sap drippings or acorns denting the top and hood. The car was always cleaned, waxed, and shiny. The license plate read, "BIG T."

Now Morgan was behind the wheel of his uncle's SUV. Bell loved it.

"Man, we're riding in style now. I bet you don't get to do this often."

"Nah," Morgan said.

Unlike Aunt Mae's car, his uncle tuned the radio to jazz. Morgan did not know this kind of music and pretended he liked it when he was a passenger in the car. Uncle T would talk about the musicians, reminiscing when he last saw them play or if he had the album. Morgan turned the volume down but not off.

He pulled into the garage. They got out and walked into the house. Bell had his possessions in a knapsack, and he followed Morgan through the kitchen and to the living room. Pictures were in frames all over the tables, and bookshelves. Bell could tell it was a home full of family memories. It's not unlike his family back home, where most pictures were of him, his sports accomplishments, and the trophies—a memory he wanted to forget now.

Aunt Mae instructed, "Mo, show Bell to the small guest bedroom."

She later brought a towel and washcloth. She would warm up the pie and fix a plate for each of them. Her pies were the best, with just the right creaminess, sweetness, and seasonings. In addition, they each had a cup of coffee or tea. This might help them get a good night's sleep.

Aunt Mae would fix breakfast in the morning before returning to the medical center. She was anxious to get back to Tre.

"Thank you, Ms. Mae." Bell appropriately thanked Aunt Mae for inviting him into her home.

Morgan and Bell left the living room, climbed the stairs, and went down the hall to the bedroom. After dropping off Bell's knapsack, they went to Morgan's room for a minute.

"Mo, I'm thankful we crossed each other's path today." As he told Morgan earlier, Bell believed God sent him to be his angel.

"I have been provided food, now a place to sleep that's not a homeless shelter, rescued from the cops, and possibly found a job. If that's not a blessing, then nothing is. Your family is kind to open their home to me, particularly under these circumstances."

Morgan interrupted Bell to say he was glad he could help him, but he was no angel.

Morgan asked, "Do your parents know where you are? Have you called them? Let them know you're safe and that you found me and we're together. It would be a relief."

"You're right," Bell replied. This would be a good time to call so they will not worry as much. At least he had some good news to tell them. Until now, he could only say he was homeless. Bell said he would call in the morning.

"Good night, my brother." Bell returned to the guest bedroom, where he would get some well-needed sleep.

Morgan realized he still needed to call KeTani. It was getting seriously late, and she would have been asleep if he did not call soon.

"Hello, beautiful."

"Hi, handsome."

He hoped she was not asleep. He proceeded to tell her about the long evening. He was sorry he could not talk earlier, but she understood how hectic it can be for a family with a loved one in dire need of medical attention. That was Mo's family.

"How is Uncle T?" asked KeTani.

"He's resting. The nurses and doctors are doing the usual monitoring protocols. He has all these wires and tubes connected to keep a watch on him. He was speaking but not able to communicate fully. The plan is to check on him tomorrow. Hopefully, the doctors will know more at that time. That will determine if he can come home to recuperate. Aunt Mae is okay. She's a strong lady who knows better than anyone he has not taken care of himself. Are you working tomorrow?

Maybe you can check in on how he's doing. I know he'd like," said Morgan.

He described the police incident. Bell was very upset by this experience. They were looking for someone who had stolen some items from a convenience store. After a brief but tense confrontation, it was a case of mistaken identity.

"Wow! That's hard to believe," said KeTani.

"I jumped into the middle of the arrest and told the cops Bell was with me."

"I heard about this on the radio," said KeTani.

"The suspect got into a physical fight with the store owner and was stabbed by the store owner before he left the store. But the robber left with $1,500 in cash. They found him at an Urgent Care facility trying to get treated for the wound. The staff called the police, and they arrived to make the arrest. That sounds exciting and yet scary at the same time."

"Yeah, I know, right. Bell is staying with us for a few days."

"What? He's staying where you are now. But aren't you moving?"

"Yes, but not until the apartment is furnished. He needed a place to stay, and Aunt Mae was the one who told him he could stay here. He will go to Grace Gardens for a job interview, and we're hoping they will hire him so he can move into his own place. Having him around will be nice for both of us. In the meantime, he won't need to go to a homeless shelter. As for me, your help is still needed. It will take a few days before I'm fully move-in ready."

Morgan let KeTani know that his parents were coming to visit the next day. After they learned about Uncle T collapsing at work and being hospitalized, they decided to come to help

Aunt Mae. He told her their offer to help get some things for the apartment. Morgan reminded her that he had not seen them since moving to Memphis. He only talked with them on the phone on occasion. It will also be an opportunity for them to meet her. Tomorrow was beginning to shape up into another busy day. He planned to pick them up at the airport midday.

"How was your day, KeTani?"

She was glad he came up for air so she could talk. She had been holding it in long enough. She had thought long and hard about what he asked her earlier and decided.

"I decided to move into the apartment," she said after a long pause.

"Are you saying yes?" Morgan asked, surprised by her change of heart.

"I am. The answer is yes."

She'd talked to her dad, and he was okay with her decision. He did ask if she was pregnant and if there were long-term plans she wanted to share.

"His rationale was that I would spend so much time over there anyway, I might as well live there."

Her decision made Morgan very happy. He started to talk about how great it would be, and that she wouldn't regret it.

KeTani jumped in. "Slow your roll. There are a few conditions."

She would move in, but not before thirty days. She wanted to give her roommates a little notice. She would lead the effort to purchase furniture and household things. Clearly, he knew nothing about apartment living, what they might need, and how to decorate the place. Morgan must promise to pick up his clothes and keep the house neat.

"When you go to Grace Gardens tomorrow, ask for a two-bedroom apartment. That way, we can use the extra room as an office/guest bedroom when family or friends visit." And finally, she would take care of the other expenses, utilities, phone, cable, and groceries, if he took care of the rent.

He was happy with whatever she wanted. Morgan was thrilled. It was the perfect end to a long, exhausting day.

He could introduce her to his parents as his roommate (and maybe girlfriend). That would be a first.

"Let's plan to see each other for dinner on Sunday because Saturday morning I'll be busy with Bell, my parents, and visiting Uncle T at the hospital."

He again told her he loved her. It would be hard for him to imagine, right now, not being with her.

"Goodnight."

Morgan thought about his day and all that had transpired. It was especially great reconnecting with Bell and getting the apartment. He was worried about Uncle T despite knowing he was receiving quality care. He was not sure what to expect from his parents coming to visit. He was overjoyed by the relationship he and KeTani were developing. He had a job that could allow him opportunities to embark on a successful career. He had a mentor in Old Man Evans. Life was beginning to look pretty damn good. It was the **best day ever.**

CHAPTER 15

Saturday Morning

They all got some needed rest after a late night of unforeseen activity. The next day, everyone took as much time as necessary to rise from bed, get dressed, and prepare for appointments.

Aunt Mae was anxious to return to the hospital to check on Tre. She needed to know what was wrong. But mainly, she wanted to be by his side so he would be comforted. She was sure he was miserable lying in bed in a hospital wearing one of those skimpy gowns. It never mattered to him if he had a little pain in his leg or arm. He would get up and get on with his day at work. Sometimes he would rub some ointment or liniment on the pain.

"Tre never stayed home when he felt a little sick," she muttered to herself. "He always thought the worst of the guys calling in sick, some frequently, claiming they needed a mental health day. That kind of thinking was not in his DNA. Tre probably got up the other morning knowing full well he was not his usual self, but he went to work anyway. If he didn't feel right, he should have stayed home."

This time, it caught up to him. The best Aunt Mae could

do now was be there by his side. So, when the nurses checked his blood pressure and temperature and looked at whatever vital measurements they were monitoring, he would not give them a difficult time. Hopefully, by the time the doctor came to check on him, he would be ready to receive the news of what was wrong. Aunt Mae was praying he could come home. If getting some rest was all he needed, he would be more relaxed at home watching sports on TV or listening to a jazz album.

Then there was Bell. He had a 10:30 AM job interview at Grace Gardens. He was somewhat nervous about the prospect, especially if he failed. But the job would provide income and permanent shelter, a way out of temporary homelessness. Morgan would need to drive him there and introduce him to Ms. June. Bell needed more experience interviewing for a job. He did not have a resume on hand. He did not work while attending high school. Those years were about playing football. As a top prospect, his time was spent in the training room when he was not playing. In college, he had a work-study job in the Athletic Department. He would hang out around the building and run errands for the department head when necessary. The job was handed to him without regard for a resume or interview.

After he came home, he received assistance getting a truck driving job. His biggest hurdle there was passing the Class D license test. Once he was certified with a CDL, he was good to go. The industry was so desperate for drivers that having no prior experience was fine. Having a solid reference was more critical, and his cousin was able to provide that.

Bell understood he would need to win over Ms. June with his personality and charm. Although he knew little about maintenance, he had to appear confident. Despite being homeless, he had to appear harmless, unlikely to annoy other people or cause concerns. As long as he had his "angel" on his side, what could go wrong?

Morgan needed to be at the airport to pick up his parents. They would be arriving around 12:30 PM. Morgan had mixed feelings about seeing them. He was a little apprehensive because it had been years since he saw them. After he moved south, he called every week. Six months later, that changed to once a month. Now, it was hardly at all. Not talking with them was his way of avoiding specific topics. He was finally ready to talk. He was also excited because he could tell everyone about KeTani and their plans for her to move into the apartment. He wanted to tell Aunt Mae and Bell this morning but would wait until his parents arrived.

Morgan's parents used to take a trip south every year. It was important for the sisters to stay in touch. Although Maggie and Mae talked with each other often, they had not seen each other for quite some time, at least more than five years. In the past, one of them would drive to visit the other, but those trips had become a thing of the past. No one wanted to drive 600 miles, and flying was too expensive. Morgan thought he would see them at least once a year. Instead, it all boiled down to occasional phone calls. No matter. They now reserved taking a trip for extraordinary or emergency circumstances. In the afternoon, Maggie and Louis would be arriving.

Bell walked into the kitchen, saying, "Good morning."

Aunt Mae responded by saying, "Yes, it is. Can I pour you some coffee, water, or juice?"

"A cup of coffee would be nice," he replied."

"Did you sleep okay?" asked Morgan.

"Yes, it was the best sleep I've had in weeks. I felt warm and safe. I surely appreciate you inviting me to stay in your home," he said, turning to Aunt Mae.

Then Bell's attention shifted to what he was smelling on the stove.

Aunt Mae had cooked an extra special breakfast that morning knowing the three of them would be somewhat tired after a challenging night.

Aunt Mae blessed the food, and they all started to chow down. As expected, she cooked the works: scrambled eggs, maple-glazed bacon, grits, a slice of melon, biscuits, and gravy. It wouldn't be Southern without the grits.

"Aunt Mae, we need to have guests more often," said Morgan. "That was one of the best breakfast meals we've had in a long time," he teased.

"You need to hush, baby," she replied. "We eat like this most of the time."

Morgan chuckled, saying, "But you don't always put your foot in it to give it that extra kick."

She repeated herself and said, "Hush."

Bell spoke up, "I don't know what you do regularly, but I know what I get to eat, and this was one of the best meals I have ever had."

"Thank you, sweetheart," Aunt Mae replied.

No one wanted to talk about the incident last night with the police, so the room got silent. When the eating was all done, they had a look on their faces of fulfillment. The meal was so filling that Morgan felt he needed to go back to sleep with a full stomach. They slowly got up from the table. The dishes, pots, and pans were cleared and cleaned. They were now ready to begin handling their business for the day.

Aunt Mae was ready to leave as soon as she could. Her mission was to check on Tre and talk with the doctors.

"Mo, we're still planning a big Sunday dinner, whether Tre is here or not. With Bell here your parents coming in today, and you getting the apartment, we have cause for a celebration. Did you invite your friend KeTani and her parents? I think it's about time we get to know her better. You okay with that?"

"Yes, Aunt Mae. That sounds wonderful."

As soon as she could, she was out the door and on her way.

* * * *

The hospital was busy as usual, but there were more visitors because it was Saturday. Aunt Mae found her way back to Tre's hospital room, where he was sitting in bed with the television playing a documentary. He was awake, but it looked like he had only been awake a few minutes.

"Hey, Tre. How are you feeling this morning? Are you comfortable? Need some water?" Mae kept asking questions before Tre could answer.

"Mae, I'm okay," Tre finally got a word in. "I want to go home to relax. I've seen plenty of nurses, each one checking a different part of my body. I'm not doing anything more than sitting in bed. I could get up to sit in the chair, but it could be more uncomfortable with all these tubes and wires. I go to sleep, and they wake me again shortly after to do another check. There's nothing to watch on TV. I understand they might not want me to go back to work immediately, but sitting here doesn't feel like it's helping me for whatever happened."

"Try to be patient," Mae urged. "You may not remember I told you last night that Maggie and Louis are visiting us. I told them you collapsed at work and were taken to the hospital."

Tre looked at her and asked, "Why did you do that? I'll be out of here and back to work this week. I don't need any extra help. Did they think I was dying, had a heart attack, or had a severe stroke?"

"Tre, that's not nice. That's my sister. She's coming to make sure I'm okay and to see if I need help. It's not always about you. It's been years since they came to see us, and I, for one, am looking forward to it. Plus, they'll spend time with Mo, who they haven't seen in such a long time. They want to help him too. If you're home, I hope you can put a smile on that twisted face of yours and at least show some appreciation for them making the trip. Now, sit still and go back to sleep or do something else other than grumble. Grumbling never helped anybody."

They sat and waited and waited some more. That's all they could do. After several hours, the doctor visited and reviewed Tre's file. He asked Tre a couple of questions and tried to assess his reactions.

"Mr. Jackson, the best we can tell is that you might have experienced dehydration. Try to drink more water during the day, fewer sweet drinks, and no alcohol. You got dizzy and fainted. Fortunately, you didn't hurt yourself when you fell. Also it looks like your blood pressure was extremely low. It would be best to see your primary care physician to address this. Finally, we noticed some swelling in your legs and ankles. Your numbers indicate you might be prediabetic. That should be checked out as well. We can let you go home, but take a few days to a week off from work to give your body a chance to recover. Give us time to process your discharge papers, and you'll be on your way. The nurse will come in to disconnect you from the IV fluids and the chest monitor."

"That's good news, doctor," Mae said. "We'll go home and have a good meal, and then I can prepare for our visitors. Oh, by the way, Mo has a friend staying with us," she informed him. "His name is Bell. Mo and he were high school friends. Somehow, they bumped into each other here. I learned that he was without a place to stay. Mo's friend, his name is Bell, has a job interview at Grace Gardens. That's where Mo will be moving into his apartment. I also asked Mo to invite his female friend and her parents for Sunday dinner. I think she is his steady girlfriend. It would be good for them to meet Mo's parents."

"I miss one night, and all this happened. So much for getting some rest. Who is the guy again, and where did he come from? Haven't we met this young lady? She's not pregnant, is she? These young folk are enjoying sex without protection and not thinking about the consequences. Now, you want to meet the parents. It would be best if you stopped meddling in his life."

"Tre, don't worry about that. You need to focus on yourself. Let's get a plan to get you healthy. You need more exercise and better eating habits."

It was another three hours before the hospital nurse said they could leave.

CHAPTER 16

Saturday Afternoon

Morgan and Bell sat in the living room to pass the time after Aunt Mae left the house. It was too early to drive over to Grace Gardens.

"Thanks again, Mo," Bell said.

Morgan responded, "For what?"

"For everything."

"Think nothing of it."

Morgan was happy that Aunt Mae offered to let Bell stay at the house. He probably wouldn't have asked her. Especially with so much on her plate, like Tre being hospitalized, Mo's parents visiting, and Mo moving out of the house. Morgan was grateful to his aunt for everything.

"And that breakfast was slamming. I don't know why you would want to leave her cooking for a bowl of cereal. You can't cook, bro. To get some eggs, grits, and bacon, if you aren't living here, you'll need to go to IHOP or some other restaurant." They both chuckled.

"So, what will I need to do to get this job that I'm not sure I can handle? Who am I meeting with? You know I'm not at all prepared for this interview," said Bell.

"Just be yourself, be confident. Tell her you're a responsible, hard-working person willing to learn. All you need to know is how to keep the place looking nice and to fix a few things. Ms. June will make you feel at ease, she's easy to talk to. Most of all, be honest. Don't try to fake it," responded Morgan. "You got this!"

Morgan wondered how many people were applying for the job. Ms. June seemed anxious about finding the right person.

"Regardless, it would be best if you got the job because it comes with an apartment."

After a few minutes, Bell blurted out, "Last night with the police was a trip." Morgan had thought that conversation was over, and it was behind both of them.

"It was, and let's not talk about it anymore. It's over, and nothing bad came of it besides our memories. Hopefully, we won't think about it too much."

"But it will always be in my memory," Bell replied. "Always."

"Let's go. We can get there early so you can see the place and know how much yard work you'll need to do around the property. Maybe we'll bump into these three ladies I saw when we were there. They live in Building C. I'm sure they will need the plumbing or air conditioner fixed. You might find this job better than you could ever imagine," joked Morgan.

Morgan was able to drive Uncle T's SUV again. It was the only reason he hoped his uncle's discharge would last a few days. They were about twenty minutes early and slowly drove around the apartment complex. There were numerous bushes and plants, far more than they could count. All those trees would drop hundreds of leaves to pick up or blow somewhere out of sight. There were five three-story buildings with about thirty-six apartments each. A part of the job would be to ensure the HVAC systems were working correctly. Even Morgan was having second thoughts. Was this too much for an onsite maintenance man?

They walked into the office. Ms. Latham was there to greet them.

"Hi, Morgan. I hope you're doing well today," she said.

"I am. I haven't moved in yet but hope to take care of that by the end of the week," he replied. "This is my close friend, Bell."

"Well, hello, young man." Ms. Latham turned her attention to him. "I understand you're looking for a job. Is that right?"

"Yes, ma'am. I just arrived in the city and need to find work. Previously, I was a truck driver."

"Let's step into my office so we can talk more. Morgan, you take a seat here in the lounge area," Ms. Latham instructed.

"Bell, you have to complete this job application," she said, handing him the forms.

After he finished filling out the paperwork, he walked into her office for the interview.

"So, your first name is Rufus, and your last name is Bellamy?"

"Yes, but I prefer you call me Bell. I never use Rufus. In school, everybody teased me about my name."

"You can call me Ms. June," she responded. "Rufus is a very common name in the South. You're more likely not to be teased around here. You didn't list an emergency contact. Is there no one?"

"I don't have any family living nearby."

"Then list Morgan. How about your most recent address?"

Bell and Ms. June talked for about thirty-five minutes. The conversation was better than he could imagine. She made it seem easy.

Morgan could not see Bell to gauge his body language. He assumed the interview was going well. Finally, the door opened, and Bell emerged with a smile on his face. He got the job! She would need to conduct a background check on any criminal record. If he passed, the job was his.

They excused themselves and headed over to look at the studio apartment in Building A. Ms. Latham asked Morgan to stay and if anyone came looking for her, tell them she would be right back.

Morgan took the time to look around a bit more. He looked at the activities calendar and other postings on the bulletin board. After five minutes, one of the three ladies he'd met the day before entered the office looking for Ms. Latham. They exchanged greetings, both recognizing each other.

"Have you moved in that fast? That was quick."

"No, not yet," responded Morgan. "By the way, I'm Morgan."

"My name is Tricia. My roommates are Tina and Tanya. We call ourselves the 3Ts."

"I should be able to remember that." Morgan answered. "If you're looking for Ms. June, she's showing an apartment to a close friend of mine. They should be back shortly."

"Is that the woman that was with you yesterday?" Tricia asked.

"No, not her. It's one of my boys from my hometown."

"Oh, in that case, I hope he's as cute as you. Things are beginning to look better around Grace Gardens." Without hesitation, she asked, "Was that your girlfriend with you yesterday?"

Mo was caught off guard.

"No, not really, we're good friends. I mean, we date."

"That's okay. You can still come over if you need help. Let Ms. Latham know I stopped by and will return later. See you around."

Why didn't he tell her the truth? He finally had a girlfriend and tried to hide it from the first lady who asked him about the relationship. That's not good.

He almost forgot to invite KeTani and her parents for Sunday dinner. He grabbed his cell phone to call her before he forgot again.

"Hey, beautiful. I hope you're well today. I may not get to see you with my busy schedule. Right now, I'm at Grace Gardens. Bell got the job, and he is taking a look at the studio apartment. How is your day shaping up?"

"Hi, handsome. I'm currently not busy. I wasn't sure if we were going shopping today."

Mo replied, "That's impossible. My parents are arriving this afternoon and will probably demand my attention."

He immediately invited KeTani and her parents for dinner tomorrow at 4:00 PM. It would be good for the parents to meet each other.

"Does that work for you?"

"Sure, I guess," KeTani replied. "That should be okay. I'll check with my father and stepmom. See you tomorrow."

Another five minutes passed, Bell and Ms. June came

through the door. Bell had an even bigger smile.

"So, let's sign these employment papers and be ready to start the following Monday. That will give you a week to settle into the apartment and find appropriate work clothes," said Ms. June to Bell.

Morgan asked Ms. June if he could talk with her about the apartment. "Of course," she answered. They both stepped into the office.

"Do you remember I was here with my lady friend yesterday? We decided, I mean, she has now decided to move into the apartment too, but not for thirty days. Will there be a two-bedroom available?"

"I have one now, but I can't hold it vacant that long," she replied. "As I mentioned yesterday, have her come by to fill out the papers. I'll hold it for one week. I won't ask for the extra deposit, but you do have to pay the additional rent amount."

"Okay," exclaimed Morgan. "Oh, I almost forgot. Tricia from Building C came by looking for you."

Morgan left Ms. Latham's office, turned to Bell, and said, "Let's go."

It was only noon, so they had two hours before they needed to arrive at the airport.

Bell had a look of pure happiness. Mo had not seen him look like this since the football team won the conference championship. He had a job and a place to stay. He just needed to figure out how to survive for a week and find money to purchase work clothes. He also needed to depend on his "angel" until he settled in and earned his first paycheck.

"Bell, one of the lovely ladies, stopped by the office as soon as you and Ms. June went to look at the apartment. Her name is Tricia. One of these days, she and her two running buddies will introduce themselves. All their first names begin with the letter T. She acted flirtatious, if you know what I mean. Suggesting that I drop by if I need anything. She saw me with KeTani and didn't seem to care."

Bell warned Mo, "She sounds like trouble. You need to be careful with a woman like that. She will certainly get you in trouble with KeTani, girlfriend or not. Stay away. Given my situation, I'm better positioned to get into trouble with these ladies." They both laughed.

"We could only be that lucky, Bell. You'll see after you meet them. It might be difficult to resist."

Morgan pulled up to the airport's curbside pickup, searching for his parents. He moved the car forward slowly, hoping to spot them.

"They won't expect being picked up in Uncle T's car, so keep a sharp lookout," said Morgan.

"There they are, Mo. Pullover."

Morgan maneuvered the car so he could get closer to where his parents were standing. He rolled down the passenger side window as they approached.

"Hello, Mr. and Mrs. Ordell. Can we give you a ride?"

They looked at Bell, and it took a moment for them to recognize Mo, especially driving Tre's luxury black SUV.

"Well, hello, Mo. What a surprise to see you driving a car like this," said his mom. "Hello, Bell. Morgan mentioned you were here, but I did not expect to see you."

His parents looked over at Morgan and walked over to give him a big hug. It didn't matter if they held up traffic. This was a moment they had been waiting for.

"How are you, Mo? You look great." His mom pointed out that he had grown a few more inches, gained a little weight, and now had facial hair."

Now it was his dad's turn. He also hugged him, something he rarely did.

"Hey, son. I'm looking forward to hearing about how it's going, your job, and moving into your first apartment. This is exciting." Morgan had never seen his dad this enthusiastic about anything he'd done.

"Mom and Dad, it's good to see you both, but we should get into the car before these airport traffic cops yell at us."

Bell loaded the suitcases in the cargo area—they climbed in the back seats. Morgan explained that Aunt Mae was at the medical center. He was to bring them to the house first and then call her to find out if they should come over or not. Those were his instructions.

"That's just like my sister, telling us where and when to go." Maggie said, "She likes to be in charge."

Bell asked about the flight. Louis responded that it was smooth flying, with no issues at the airport and no loss of luggage. Considering how bad it could be, he gave it an excellent rating. But now he was ready for something to eat and a place to relax.

"So, Bell, what brings you here?"

"Mrs. Ordell, it's a long story."

Mo knew he did not want to tell the whole story because he was embarrassed. Instead, Bell told her his travels brought him here and reunited him with his good friend Mo, and everything had already been a blessing. Mo observed that his mother could not follow that response with more questions.

She had not expected that kind of answer. She does not remember any of his friends being committed to their faith. Usually, it was the opposite. He ensured his mom knew that Bell was staying at the house for now, but "today he got a job and a place to live."

They pulled into the driveway, got out, and entered the house. Mo's mother knew which bedroom to go to. She placed the luggage and changed her shoes to something more comfortable. They all gathered back in the kitchen.

Morgan grabbed his cell phone to call Aunt Mae.

"Hi, we're at the house. How's it going at the medical center? How's Uncle Tre?"

"He's doing well," replied Mae. "They are working on the discharge papers, and he can go home. It's better if everyone stays there. Ask Maggie to fix some sandwiches. You'll find some deli meats in the fridge and sub rolls in the bread basket. I will talk with everyone when I get home."

"Okay, thanks." Mo relayed the instructions. They each had a sandwich, some chips, and soda or water.

Mo and Bell passed the time listening to Mo's parents talk about how much had changed back home. There are new restaurants, and some familiar places could be better. He got updated on who got married, had a new baby, graduated from college, and died among their friends. Most of the information sounded like gossip—one story after another. Morgan hadn't noticed during all that, but Bell had left the room for a few minutes and then returned.

"My parents say hello to everyone," Bell stated. "I hadn't talked with them in a couple of weeks. They were pleased that I was staying with Mo and his family. They were delighted that

I have a new job."

Finally, after a few more minutes, Aunt Mae opened the door. Uncle T was behind her, walking in slowly as if he had aged a few years overnight.

"We're home." Aunt Mae was thrilled to see and hug her sister. The men all gave a brotherly handshake and a pat on the back. There's so much to talk about and discuss. It was shaping up to be a long night. Before Mo could call it a night, he had to do one thing, clean Uncle T's car, wipe it down both inside and out, and vacuum the carpet.

That evening Aunt Mae fixed another delicious meal. She always cooked extra fixings when visitors are around. Morgan was unsure when she had the time to cook, including the bread pudding, but everything was delicious. She wanted it special for her sister. Not having Tre at the hospital made it easier for her to concentrate on making a hearty meal. Throughout dinner, the older adults kept bombarding Mo and Bell with questions. They wanted to know what brought Bell to Memphis. He could no longer respond that it was a long story. They were ready to listen and had the time. He would be sure not to share anything about the two men who attacked him. He kept that a secret.

Bell told them about being fired while coming to the close of a major haul.

"How could they just terminate you while on the road?" Louis remarked. "That's horrible. You should get a lawyer and request additional compensation. Normally, you can get some severance pay when you're released without cause."

Bell had no plans to seek retribution. He felt lucky to have the job. He focused on finding what was next, provided he could escape the hole he found himself in.

"It's great that you are here, and for you and Mo to accidentally see each other is amazing," said Maggie.

"What a blessing." Bell looked at Mo and smiled.

"Did you know Mo had moved here?"

"No, I knew he moved south, but not the place," Bell answered.

They kept asking him about homelessness and how he managed it for the last few weeks. They then moved on to Morgan, asking him about the apartment. How much space? Why did he feel he needed a two-bedroom? What furniture did he need, and where would he get it? Each one had advice about living in an apartment. For them, that was more than twenty-five years ago. Morgan politely listened while thinking of how outdated their input sounded. He could only listen since he had no idea what to expect. Yesterday, he had no idea what to expect.

His parents also wanted to know something about KeTani. Morgan answered by telling them they'd meet her the following day.

Morgan stated, "I know you'll find her very attractive. She is even more brilliant," he added. "More importantly, she's the best friend I got."

"More than me," interrupted Bell.

"Yes, more than you."

Morgan asked his parents about the black pouch. Aunt Mae handed it to him yesterday, but he still didn't know how to open it.

"Yes, you do, Mo," they both said simultaneously. "What did we repeatedly rehearse with you when you ran track?" He then remembered they would shout the countdown, 3 – 2 – 1. He was also to use that as an emergency code if he were ever in trouble. He was to leave those numbers in a voice message or text them if he needed help.

"We just knew you would never forget."

He realized the irony of the situation that this was to help him when he was least in need of help.

"I'll take a look inside before I go to bed tonight."

Finally, they focused on Tre. Aunt Mae was very anxious about having a plan of action to make sure he got plenty of rest and was fully recuperated before returning to work. Each of them took turns talking about their various aches and pains. The topic of discussion moved between the problems with the back to the legs, worrying about weight gain and loss, and all the medications they were taking to address all kinds of ailments. Morgan and Bell were happy they were not having these issues, but more importantly, the conversation shifted away from them—no more questions.

CHAPTER 17

Church & Sunday Dinner

Before they said goodnight, they agreed to attend church at Land of Beulah Baptist Church. This was not Aunt Mae's regular church, a Church of God in Christ church. Service began at 10:00 AM. They had enough time for a quick breakfast. Morgan knew he needed a strong cup of coffee to help keep him awake during the sermon. With six people in the house, they took turns using the two bathrooms to get ready. Since Bell had very few clothes and nothing considered church-going, they had to find something for him to wear from Uncle T's wardrobe. They were entirely outdated, but that was the best they could do. Per the doctor's order, Uncle T would stay at home. Aunt Mae, Maggie, Louis, Bell, and Morgan got in the car and drove to church.

They arrived with plenty of time to find seats about ten rows from the front. The congregants were all moving about the sanctuary. Many of them were regular church-going folks who knew each other. They were all giving each other hugs, kisses, and handshakes. You could hear them affirming what each person was saying by the frequent calling out of amen or praise God. It was a family-like atmosphere.

Morgan thought they must have stood out as visitors because they just sat down and were not being greeted or greeting anyone. He gazed around to see if he recognized anyone from work but didn't. He also noticed that the church was filled mainly with the elderly. So where were the young adults, people his age? A few children sat with an adult, and a few served as ushers or worship leaders who seemed middle-aged. But where was his age group? Then he noticed a group sitting together near the back on the right side.

Like Morgan, most young adults stopped going to a traditional church. Generally, the music was bland and from the old hymnals. The sermons were always about sinners. That negativity was constant and fell on deaf ears. More importantly, many young adults viewed the church as hypocritical. They would notice folks praising God on Sunday and acting un-Christlike the rest of the week. They attended church services that felt more authentic. He believed churches needed to break away from the same old thing every week. With a closer look at the group in the back, he noticed the guys were not wearing ties, and the ladies wore slacks and not dresses. That's a change. He and his friends always talked about feeling welcomed and not judged. Maybe today, he would develop a positive spirit.

The music finally started, and it had a nice, almost danceable feel. The music was not supposed to feel like a nightclub or concert, but it was always nice to have something that made you move. Everyone stood up, clapped, and sang the words. Those who stood had that gospel sway from side to side. The organ, piano, bass, and drums with guitars and a saxophone player accompanied the music. The choir was an ensemble of twelve talented voices. Each one could seriously sing, and they took turns as soloists. After the announcements and a prayer, the choir sang one of Maggie's favorite songs by Edwin Hawkins titled "Changed." She would play that song over and over again, singing along as if no one was listening. When the song was done, women screamed, standing up with their arms reaching upward. Morgan looked at his mom. She had a tear dripping down her face. Morgan glanced at his friend Bell, who seemed caught up in the emotion.

The preacher stood up and approached the pulpit. He cleared his voice before speaking and said which Bible verse he would use for his sermon. He recited Isaiah, Chapter 41, verses 10-11:

10 So do not fear, for I am with you;
do not be dismayed, for I am your God.
I will strengthen you and help you;
I will uphold you with my righteous right hand.

11 All who rage against you
will surely be ashamed and disgraced;
those who oppose you
will be as nothing and perish.

His sermon title was, "Be In Courage." The meaning was to be ready and willing to face adverse situations and, in doing so, to place your trust in the Lord as your source of strength. It was an appropriate message for what had happened the day prior and something to live by going forward.

Morgan observed his family and friend to catch a glimpse of how they were receiving the message. They all nodded their heads to affirm what the preacher was saying. Occasionally, he would hear someone say, "That's right," or "Tell it, Pastor," as if he needed more encouragement to deliver the word.

Morgan was pleased the sermon was only thirty minutes long. It must be because of the football game at 1:00 PM. Lord knows some preachers can unapologetically go on for forty-five minutes or more. The sermon was over, they passed the offering plate around for contributions, and the congregants were dismissed in the usual manner. The family slowly walked out of the church, shaking hands with the pastor and a member of the deacon board. They said to each of them, "Please come back." Morgan could tell the pastor was not familiar with anyone in his family.

In the car, everyone expressed how lovely the service was and how much they needed that message. Morgan could hear his mom humming today's song. It will probably be in her head for the whole week. When they returned to the house, they went to their respective bedrooms to change clothes and get slightly more comfortable.

Soon, it would be dinner time, and the Mason family would arrive for a get-to-know-you meal. Aunt Mae and Maggie immediately went to the kitchen to cook, Morgan and Bell disappeared upstairs, and Uncle Tre and Louis sat in front of the TV to watch the football game. Morgan was a little nervous about the dinner as he prepared to inform his family that KeTani was moving in with him. Since Mr. Mason already knew, telling them before she and her folks arrived might be best. He decided to tell Bell first to practice his answers to any questions.

"So, Bell. You should know that KeTani and I plan to live

together at the apartment. It didn't start out that way, but we discussed it, and it made sense." He paused so Bell could ask him a question. But he did not.

"That sounds great, Mo. You two have been together for a few years. I can't recall you ever having a steady girl. So why not share a place to live." Bell was not much help for a practice round.

He had yet to share this information with the family. He must tell them before the guests arrive.

"She must be an exceptional lady for you to take this kind of step," said Bell.

"She is," Morgan answered. He had never felt this way before, but he guessed it was what love felt like. He couldn't imagine not being with her. When they were together, everything felt great, better than being with a best friend. Neither was ready for marriage or anything like that, more like roommates with benefits.

As Bell pointed out, Morgan couldn't cook that well. He was horrible at keeping a room neat and organized, let alone an entire apartment. All the things about managing a household, she would provide. Don't get him wrong. He was not looking for a homemaker. He expected to learn a lot from her, which would help him manage things better. It would give them a chance to be together more often and feel the comfort of home.

Bell asked, "Why are you explaining your relationship with KeTani and looking for justification? It all sounds good to me. You don't need my approval. As a matter of fact, you don't need approval from anyone but hopefully, you receive positive feedback."

Morgan was ready to share his big news. Hopefully, his

parents would understand and agree. He desperately wanted their support. Morgan first went into the kitchen, where the ladies were preparing dinner.

"Mom, Aunt Mae, how's it going?

"We're doing fine," they both responded in unison.

"That's good. I want our guests to enjoy this visit. This will be your first time meeting my girlfriend, KeTani."

Aunt Mae turned around and repeated, "Girlfriend? When did this happen? Yesterday, you were just friends."

Maggie looked at him with a smile and said, "It's nice to have a person you're regularly dating. I'm sure she's a nice person. I can hardly wait to meet her."

Morgan immediately said, "We plan to live in the apartment together. She already told her roommates that she's moving out. She also told her dad and stepmother."

"Now I really want to meet this young lady who will be living with my son. She'd better be more than just nice," his mom responded. "It's a surprise but I'm glad you told us, son."

"Me too," chimed in Aunt Mae.

Maggie looked at her sister for any signs of concern about the arrangement, especially because she hadn't met the young lady. Nothing seemed bothersome.

"We've dated for a few years, and I genuinely like her."

"Like or love, son? You do understand that we plan to help purchase items for the apartment, right?"

Morgan responded. "Yes."

"Now we need to discuss this with the two of you."

"I guess so," said Morgan. It was unclear why his mom would bring that up. He was convinced KeTani would handle the situation fine.

Morgan dismissed himself and went into the living room to let his dad and Uncle T know who was coming for dinner. He sat on the couch beside his dad. Uncle T was in his favorite chair with his feet on the ottoman. They were watching a football game on the television and sipping whisky. Bell was also in the room, sitting in another chair and looking at the game intensely.

"So, who is playing?" Morgan asked.

"Those dreaded New England Patriots and Dallas. I hope the Cowboys kick their butts today. I can't stand the Patriots. I generally root against the Cowboys, but today against this opponent, I want them to win," Uncle T was vehement.

"Dad…"

"Yes, son."

"We have guests coming over for dinner."

He again replied, "I know, son."

"The young lady is KeTani. She's my girlfriend."

"That's great, son," he muttered.

"She's bringing her father and stepmother with her."

"Okay." It became clear to Morgan that he did not have his full attention. The football game was more important at the moment. He could wait to tell him more, but KeTani and her family might arrive.

"KeTani and I plan to move into the apartment together," Morgan said and then paused.

"That's fine. I hope she's not pregnant, or you plan to have children or something stupid like that before you get married."

"No drastic news like that," Morgan replied. "We don't have any marriage plans. What else is stupid like that?"

No response from his dad.

"We like each other a lot and decided this arrangement works best. I'll let you continue watching the game. Maybe we can talk more about it later. I want your advice."

His dad turned to look directly at him. He heard what Morgan had said and was happy for him. He suggested they talk about things in more detail later. He was not worried and suspected Morgan was making a wise decision. He told Morgan he was smart and, honestly, not likely to take unnecessary risks like he would have done. His dad might have suggestions about how to build a long relationship. He and Maggie had been married for twenty-five years.

"We will probably have more to discuss when you're ready for the next step in this relationship." His dad continued, "We named you after the jazz trumpeter Lee Morgan. Do you know the story of how he died?"

Morgan shook his head no.

"Lee was a great musician whose life ended at the young age of 33. He played with Art Blakey, the Jazz Messengers, John Coltrane, Hank Mobley, Wayne Shorter, and many other giants."

He didn't expect him to know all those jazz giants.

"Lee Morgan's common-law wife Helen shot him in cold blood between sets at Slugs' Saloon in New York City after a confrontation. It's a tragic ending. You bear his name as a tribute to him and his music. He is the primary reason I listen to jazz today. His song, *The Sidewinder*, was highly popular. That song made the Billboard Charts Hot List. Although it was jazz, we played it at house parties. It was so good that some believe it saved the Blue Note label from going out of business. Since then, I have been drawn to all the artists on that record label and jazz music period. Why am I talking about Lee Morgan? The best advice I can give you is not to anger your spouse. If it's not working, get out of the relationship peacefully. Now let me get back to the game. We can discuss your plans later or another day while we're in town."

* * * *

A little after 4 PM, KeTani, her father, Kenneth, and his new wife, Jill, arrived. They made introductions of the parents, Maggie and Louis. He also introduced Aunt Mae and Uncle Tre, and his friend Bell. After a brief conversation with everyone, they sat down for a Sunday dinner. The spread was like one of those holiday dinners. Aunt Mae went all out for the occasion. What a treat! KeTani and Mo looked at each other and smiled.

They ate, talked, and had a good time. The parents took turns sharing stories of their past as kids and newlyweds. Some of them were downright hilarious. They seemed to get along, and that was important to Mo and KeTani. This was a day to remember, one to capture.

CHAPTER 18

Monday Blues

It was Monday morning, and Morgan was headed back to work. He could drive Uncle T's car for the third straight day. Morgan arrived at his usual time, just before 11:00 AM. He said good morning to everyone he passed on the way to his work area and retrieved his schedule for the day. He noticed that people were not in the best of spirits. He had no idea what might have happened. He thought Monday morning blues must be contagious. Usually, he would be greeted by everyone with a simple hello. This morning they all asked how he was feeling. Did they all know his parents had come to town?

A note was in his mailbox that instructed him to go to the Personnel Office as soon as he got the message. He immediately headed there rather than to the O.R. staff room. This can't be good. *Am I being fired?* His most recent review was very positive. He got along exceptionally well with his supervisor and co-workers. He had not heard of any cutbacks due to financial reasons. *Did I make an error that resulted in the loss of a patient's life?*

Morgan had a bad feeling. It felt like being called to the

principal's office. *Did this have something to do with last night when Uncle T was here and the police attempt to arrest Bell?*

He stopped in to see the office manager. There he was handed an envelope with the marking from a law firm.

"For me?" he asked.

He immediately became concerned, thinking he was in serious trouble, and some patient named him in a lawsuit. That would be a nightmare. Morgan had heard stories about staff being named in charges against a doctor performing surgery. These matters take years to be settled as the staff assisting in the procedure find life unsettling. For the first time, he felt his life was headed in the right direction. He was unprepared for any significant setback. He slowly opened the envelope and began to read.

The letter informed him that he was designated Evan Deveaux's estate executor. He wondered who the hell this person was. Was this a prank being played on him by his coworkers? Then it dawned on him that Deveaux must be Old Man Evans' last name. He had always assumed that Evans was his last name, not first. Then he read it again, and the words, *with the passing of…*, stuck out. It hit him hard. This meant he died. He looked up at the office manager as if to say it couldn't be true.

She looked at him and said, "Morgan, what's wrong?"

He handed her the letter so she could read it for herself.

"Morgan, I'm so sorry for your loss. I didn't know you two were related."

"We're not," he replied.

"But here, it states you're the executor, responsible for managing his affairs. Do you know if he had any other family members? I can check his personnel file to see if he listed anyone. But I'm not aware of any spouse or children."

The office manager went to the files, and there was no indication of any family member, just this law firm, in case of an emergency. In his will, he designated an executor should he die.

"When did this happen? I just spoke with him last week. He didn't seem sick," Morgan said.

He remembered Old Man Evans had a cough, but don't we all cough every day? The office manager suggested he contact the law firm to find out more.

"Let us know what you need. You can take personal leave time to handle this matter."

Morgan left the office to find a quiet location where he could call the law firm. After a few rings, an automated voice answered, asking for an extension. Morgan had a name, but that's it. Finally, he reached the receptionist.

"Hello, can I speak to Mr. Anderson? He sent a letter to my place of employment, so I'm calling."

"Please hold. I'll see if he's available," she said.

After a few minutes, a voice answered.

"Who is this, and how can I help you?"

"My name is Morgan Ordell. I received your letter regarding Evan Deveaux's passing, and your message said he designated me as his executor."

"Yes, Mr. Ordell." Morgan rarely gets referred to as mister. "I'm sorry for your loss. I'm glad you received the letter and called me. Mr. Deveaux had me draw up his Will a few weeks ago. It would be good for you to come to the office to discuss it."

"Yes, sir," Morgan replied. "What did he die from? When and where did this occur?"

"It happened on Friday around 5:00 PM. He had just left work and was on his way to his apartment. He stopped to sit on the bench at the bus stop. When a bus pulled up, he continued to sit there. Finally, someone noticed he did not get up when a second bus arrived. He was found dead, sitting on the bench. I believe he had a heart attack."

"If you can come into my office this week, I can go over his estate in detail and assist you with the probate court process if you wish us to handle it. When are you available?"

"How about this afternoon?" Morgan replied.

"That can work. Is 3:00 PM okay?"

"Yes, sir."

"Great. See you then."

Morgan left the Personnel Office and was at a loss for what to do. He wanted space and time to grieve. Old Man Evans was such a nice person. He had not realized how important he was to him. With no mentor around, he became that person Morgan went to for advice. Most of the time, they talked about life, all the twists and turns due to unexpected circumstances. This was one of them.

It was a sad story. Getting old can sometimes leave a person without anyone around to call family. Old Man Evans never talked about his friends, either. As Morgan thought about him, he realized how important coming to work must have been for him.

Work was the place where he had contact with other people. If he stayed at home, he would be in a lonely state of mind. Being at work kept him busy, gave him purpose, and exercised his mind, if not his body. Morgan began to think about his parents as they aged. He hoped they would not find themselves in a similar situation.

I guess that's why parents cherish the moments they have with their children and grandchildren. As you age, you want them nearby so they can care for you and everything you leave behind. Morgan had no idea Old Man Evans was sick. He was never absent or not feeling well. Maybe he just kept that to himself, thought Morgan.

"How could this happen? His life should not have ended this way. I never got to thank him or say goodbye."

He was torn between taking the rest of the day off or toughing it out at work. If he went home, he could spend time with his parents. If he continued working, he wondered whether he could keep his mind on this job and not drift off into thinking about his mentor. Since he had not started the work day, he decided to take the day off.

Before leaving the medical center, he informed co-workers who had not heard of Old Man Evans' passing. A few people already knew, but most had not heard anything. He told KeTani and let her know he was heading home. KeTani asked what she could do to help. He responded that he needed time to think about it. He was not sure what he must do to manage someone else's affairs. Morgan was challenged to manage his own. He had never thought about anything like this before. What does it mean to be the executor? All he could imagine was the person's personal items, and financial affairs would be managed. It was not clear to Morgan how outstanding bills got paid, and the remaining funds distributed to beneficiaries.

Morgan pulled the car into the driveway at home and

entered the front door. Everyone looked at him with surprise.

"What happened? Why are you home?" His parents, aunt, and uncle all asked in different ways.

"Is everything okay? You didn't have an accident, did you?

"No. Nothing like that," he responded.

After a brief pause, Morgan answered the barrage of questions.

"I may not have ever mentioned this guy I met at work. He died on Friday. We all called him Old Man Evans. He was much older than most of us at the medical center. He became my mentor, an adult I could talk to about everything. He always had a positive outlook on life and offered me some meaningful advice on several subjects. His real name is Evan Deveaux, and he designated me as the executor of his estate."

They were stunned by the news and unsure what to make of it. Tre worried it could be a scam. Be careful. Morgan didn't think so. He showed them the letter.

"I made an appointment today to see the lawyer to review his Will. Maybe someone here can go with me?"

Morgan wondered how he became the only person Old Man Evans would trust to give the responsibility of the estate executor. It made him think about what plans, if any, his parents had for him.

"Mom, do you and dad have a Will?"

"Mo, we each have one," she responded. "It's what you must do if you have personal property and many possessions. Louis is my designee, then Mae is the contingency."

Morgan had never thought about these matters as related to his parents. Although his parents lived a distance away, Morgan always knew they were there if he needed them.

Having this conversation was creepy. He was trying not to process this too much.

Maggie asked, "Any idea how large an estate he has? What are you expecting he left to inherit?"

"I don't know any of these answers," said Morgan. "It can't be much. Maybe we'll find out at the law firm."

* * * *

"Mr. Anderson? I'm Morgan Ordell. This is my mother, Mrs. Ordell."

"Hi, young man, ma'am. Welcome to the law office of Karl Anderson, Esq. Please have a seat in our conference room."

They all sat at a large table with fine leather chairs. There was artwork on the wall and a huge window that looked out on the city landscape.

Maggie spoke up, "My first question is, why my son, Morgan?"

Mr. Anderson explained that Mr. Deveaux had no family members to manage his affairs. He had married and divorced years ago. He had no idea where his ex-wife lived or whether she was remarried. Per his instructions, he wanted her not to receive anything from his estate. They did not have any children. His brother passed away a few years ago. It's unclear if his brother had children, but if so, they had a minimal relationship with Mr. Deveaux.

"Therefore, he decided to leave everything to you, young man."

"That means there might be nieces or nephews who feel they have the rights to his estate, correct?"

"That's right, Mrs. Ordell." As the lawyer who wrote this Will, we would fight any challenge on your behalf. Mr. Deveaux was of sound mind and clear in his instructions."

"We can review Mr. Deveaux's estate and provide information to help guide you through the probate court process. If you have questions, we can provide legal advice. Our firm knows the state laws and how the system works. However, if the estate is fundamental and not very large, you might be capable of managing this without a lawyer."

The lawyer was losing Morgan. Too much legalese. The tasks sounded overwhelming. Morgan hoped to leave with a list of what to do and where to go. Instead, he was getting a sales pitch to hire the law firm to manage the process.

Morgan interrupted, telling the lawyer he had never done this before and had no idea of the responsibilities. Mr. Anderson pointed out an executor's guidebook that would lead Morgan through the legal procedures and terminology.

"If I need your help, what will it cost?" asked Morgan.

"That depends on the state of affairs," the lawyer answered.

"Where did Evan live, and how do I get inside to see what personal items he has? Where is the body? Am I responsible for the funeral service?"

The attorney said most people use the insurance payout to cover those expenses.

"Let us help get copies of the death certificate," he said.

"How much is the insurance policy?" Mae asked.

"I believe it's $25,000," responded the lawyer.

After listening to Mr. Anderson, Maggie spoke up. "Am I to believe my son is the only person, according to the Will, to inherit this estate?"

"Yes, at the moment, ma'am. The court procedures require you, as the executor, to publicly post an announcement in the newspaper about his death. This allows anyone with a claim to file an appeal with the court. Our firm will attest that Mr. Deveaux appeared sane and was not under any pressure when he filed this Will."

"How long can this process take?"

"Months, a year, dependent upon how much we find by going through his papers, accounts, and personal belongings."

Morgan talked with Mr. Anderson for at least forty-five minutes, asking questions. He needed time to think, plan, and do whatever required action. Most of all, he needed help from his family and friends.

He and Maggie left the office to drive back home. Maggie kept reassuring him that he could do this, whatever it took. His mind was racing with all these jumbled-up thoughts. Morgan was thinking more about the sudden death of a friend. He must plan a memorial service in the chapel at the medical center. That would be his first step. Then he could concentrate on the other matters at hand. He could check to see if the body was being held at the morgue. Morgan had never been to that area of the medical center before, and he wouldn't be going there today.

This was now another distraction from moving. This became another level of responsibility he was not prepared for. His mind was racing, trying to reflect on all his conversations with Old Man Evans. He could not recall him ever saying anything about being ill or not feeling well. As far as Morgan was concerned, his mentor would live forever.

Mid-Week

Most of the family had tasks to accomplish over the next few days. There would not be time for them to hang out, other than Tre who would be recuperating, and Louis who volunteered to keep him company.

Bell got up early to venture out to Grace Gardens to get a good feel for the place. He had to get there by bus and on foot, which would help him learn how to get around and where to find things. He could hardly wait to begin work so he could earn some wages. After talking to his parents over the weekend, they quickly sent funds to his bank account. This meant he would not panhandle on street corners or have to beg for food. His stay with Morgan temporarily provided him with healthier meals and a comfortable bed for sleeping. The last few days, he went shopping for clothes, primarily for work and other items. He now had enough to last until his first paycheck.

His first stop was to see Ms. June. She was surprised to see him but pleased that he took the initiative to orientate himself to the community.

"Good morning, Bell," she said. "Do you need some assistance with anything?"

"No, ma'am." He had a small office where files were kept, a phone, a small work desk and an array of small tools. Next to his workspace was a large room for cleaning and gardening supplies, extensive tools, a sink, and buckets. He was well-equipped for the job. He would be okay figuring things out by himself.

There were four buildings with twelve apartments on each of the three floors. It was your basic living arrangement. As he walked around, he noticed several of the residents out for walks. There was a couple with a toddler, a single mom with an infant, and an elderly couple all getting some exercise. The grounds were well kept. A lawn company comes weekly to mow, trim, prune, and fertilize the plants. The landscaping was well-designed, and the place looked like it was cared for by professional workers. Fortunately, his job was to oversee their work and ensure they handled any immediate issues.

When he got over near Building C, he spotted three ladies hanging out around the building entrance.

This must be the ladies Morgan kept mentioning, he thought.

In his best suave voice, Bell said, "Hello, ladies. Enjoying the day?"

Tina responded, "We are, and it just got better."

"I'm Tricia. This is Tina, and she's Tanya. We're the Three T's. You must be Bell, Morgan's friend."

Bell quickly responded, "Yes, I am." "Have you been living here awhile?"

"Going on one year."

"Have you moved in yet?" One of the Ts asked.

"Sort of, but I don't start work until Monday. I'm the new facilities manager. I have an apartment in Building A."

Tricia was the leader of this pack.

She said, "You should drop by later. We're having a few friends over to celebrate Tina's birthday."

"Well, happy birthday."

"Thank you. It'll be easy to find us. Follow the music."

"Okay, maybe I will drop over."

Bell moved on to stick to his original plan, which was to learn the layout of the place. Morgan was right, he said to himself. They were all cute and sexy. Bell was excited about possibly going to the birthday party. It would be a chance to meet some new people and get to know these ladies.

He continued his stroll and looked at his apartment again to determine how much furniture he might need. The studio was sparsely furnished. He was surprised that it already had a bed, a couch, and a kitchen table with two chairs. There was a small bathroom and several closets—just enough and much more than he had a few weeks ago. Bell went back to see Ms. June and asked her about the furniture.

"The previous manager left it behind, so you're welcome to it," she told him.

"Thanks," he acknowledged.

"I don't know if you noticed, but pots, pans, and cooking utensils are in the cabinets and drawers. Do you cook, Bell?"

"No, not really, but I will manage."

Managing was an understatement. He ate frozen dinners or pre-packaged meals. Other than cereal in the morning, he would need help cooking an egg for breakfast. Before now, he lived at home. Bell mostly ate sandwiches on a roll or from a local sub shop. He had never gone grocery shopping and had yet to learn how to prepare or season chicken or steak. He planned to get help or spend hours at the apartment of Morgan and KeTani.

Bell was thinking about the birthday party and having second thoughts. He just met these ladies and was not really sure he would like them or enjoy hanging out with any of them. As Morgan said, they like to flirt. He was worried about how he was dressed. He wore a pair of jeans and a T-shirt, very different from what he would typically wear. He also wanted to avoid putting himself in a position where other people looked down on him because he was the facilities manager. He realized that some of the other guests might also live in the apartment complex. That could be good. It provided a way to meet other people living there.

Bell finally decided to go. He built enough nerve to check out the 3 T's. What else did he have going on?

At about 5:00 PM, Bell knocked on the door of apartment #22 to see if the invitation was for real. The door opened, and a dude was there.

"What's up?" The guy at the door asked.

"Hi, uh, I was, uh, looking for Tricia."

"Really. I'm Jerrold, Tricia's boyfriend," as his eyes looked Bell over.

"What do you want with her?"

"I'm the new facilities manager for Grace Gardens. She told me to stop by. Maybe she had something she needed me to fix." Bell tried to cover up his reasons for coming.

Jerrold asked, "Where are your tools?"

Bell knew that was not the situation, and he was there to enjoy the party. He shrugged his shoulders.

"I'm unsure what that might be, but let me ask her," Jerrold told him. "Stay here. I'll be right back."

Bell could see the birthday decorations, food, and wine on the table. The music was louder than it should be. I'm sure it was disturbing the other residents in the building. The boyfriend returned in a few minutes.

"The air conditioner problem has been resolved," he said. Thanks for stopping by." He then proceeded to close the door in Bell's face. Bell knew there wasn't a problem to be fixed. Jerrold was clearly sending a message that he was not welcome. Bell stopped the door from shutting and told Jerrold he didn't need to slam the door.

"This is a private gathering," said Jerrold. "You're the maintenance man. I don't believe you're on the guest list. Please excuse me, but step away from the door before I shut it."

Bell was startled initially, but then he had to think about what had happened. Did he misread the situation? Maybe she was not interested in him but instead just being friendly. Maybe the boyfriend overreacted and imagined he was trying to hit on his girl. Regardless, Bell remembered that running after these ladies was precisely the kind of trouble he did not need. It would be better to walk away and forget about the party. Better yet, forget about these ladies, period. He was not sure what her game was, but to not acknowledge his invitation felt like a prank. He will be sure to mention it the next time he saw her.

* * * *

KeTani and Mrs. Ordell drove to Grace Gardens to look at the apartment. They decided it would be better to determine the right furniture and décor together. Maggie was also using this as an opportunity to evaluate her son's girlfriend. She had never been confronted with this situation before. They had to turn in the key to Unit #33 in Building C and pick up the keys for the two-bedroom unit in Building B. Maggie admired the place for its design and attractiveness. The jury was still out on KeTani. Her every move and words were being scrutinized.

They opened the door, and the place smelled of cleaning products. The odor was so strong that they covered their noses and immediately walked to the sliding balcony door to let in some fresh air. Once the air cleared, they could look at the layout, make mental notes about the size and shape, and discuss what might work best and where to place things.

Maggie asked KeTani, "Why do you need two bedrooms? Will you be sleeping in separate rooms?"

"Sometimes, we need a place to work at home, so we thought this would be an office but also have a day bed so guests could sleep there," KeTani replied.

"That makes sense," Maggie said.

They looked in the kitchen cabinets, drawers, and closets. With more knowledge of the space, they could go purchase any remaining and needed items.

"I'm so glad you're here with me, Mrs. Ordell. Having a second opinion is helpful."

"I'm happy too, KeTani," Maggie answered.

They agreed for large items to be delivered on Friday. Smaller items, they would carry and drop off at the apartment. They worked on arranging the electric, cable, and internet services. All of them were placed under KeTani's name.

Once that was done, they stopped at a small deli to grab a

bite. KeTani was a little curious about Mo's relationship with his parents. He seldom talked about them. Given her relationship with her stepmother, she wondered if Morgan was close to his mother.

"Mrs. Ordell," KeTani said, "Did you miss Mo being here and away from home?"

"Of course, dear," she answered. "We expected him not to live at home, but this is a lot farther from where we live. It was a blessing that Mae was willing to have him come here. I'm sure Mo let you know we were unhappy about his decision not to attend college. That created a lot of heated discussions at home."

KeTani responded, saying, "Yes, he did share that information. It was probably a good decision at the time. He was not ready for college. I'm hopeful he'll go to school at some point. He needed time to figure it out. He must further his education if he has any ambition to advance at work."

"I guess you're right," replied Maggie.

"Are you happy about what he has done with his life?" KeTani asked.

"I'm glad to see that he has a good job, that he's in good health, and that he has such a lovely girlfriend."

"Thank you, Mrs. Ordell. You should also know that my decision to move into the apartment was not an easy one to make. I wanted to spend more time with him and knew I was interested in being together. We're hoping it's the right thing to do. We have no delusions about marriage or having children. We'll find out if this relationship can work before we go down that pathway," said KeTani.

Maggie was impressed by her answers and her positive

attitude. She felt KeTani had her head on straight and genuinely cared for her son. She would not be mooching off her son since she had a good job. Regarding the parents, the father was kind, but like KeTani, she was uncertain about the stepmother.

There was nothing more KeTani and Maggie could do today, but they agreed to come back to vacuum, mop, and sanitize the entire apartment before permanently moving in. They were concerned about who or what was previously living there. The owners send in a cleaning company and while the cleaning job was adequate, it could've been better. With KeTani working in healthcare, she knew how germs, bacteria, and viruses could be present. She wanted it to be the nicest-looking apartment when they were done.

They traded cooking recipes for the rest of the afternoon and chatted about various television shows they watched. By the end of the afternoon, they were like mother and daughter. KeTani dropped Maggie back at the house, and she went about her own business.

CHAPTER 20

The Deveaux Estate

Morgan went with Aunt Mae to the funeral home in the neighborhood. It was used almost exclusively by her church. They discussed the process and burial costs with the funeral director. Morgan was not yet armed with a death certificate but had a letter from the law firm identifying him as the authorized person to handle Mr. Deveaux's affairs. These were both required so the funeral home could retrieve the body from the morgue.

Morgan did not know Old Man Evans' preferences should he die. This was not something they talked about. Their discussions were much more focused on living.

The funeral director asked, "Do you know if he wanted to be buried in a casket or for the body to be cremated? Do you know where you would want to bury the remains or whether you'll dispose of the remains? Will there be a service in a church, at the funeral home, or somewhere else? If you don't know the answers today, let us know. In the meantime, we should focus on transferring the body from the morgue."

Funeral home directors always have that somber look and, at the same time, seem to enjoy their work. They are part salespersons, having you decide how you will be packaged, in metal or wood, what kind of design, basic or luxury, depending on the budget. Morgan did not know how much to spend or his limit. He was being asked too many questions while grieving the loss of his trusted friend.

Morgan looked at Mae to say, help, please. He was still trying to figure out what should be done.

Mae asked the director, "Can you give us a moment to discuss all this?"

He left the room so they could talk. Morgan expressed how overwhelmed he was feeling. Mae could not imagine how he felt.

"You know him and respect this person, but he is not family."

"But Aunt Mae," Mo interrupted. "He has no one else to take care of this. This can't be left to the state and have him anonymously buried somewhere. Let's have the funeral home obtain the death certificate."

She reminded him that he must obtain proper documents that gave him the authority to make certain decisions. They asked the director to join them again. Morgan decided to have the funeral home request the death certificates from the medical examiner and transfer the body. He thought cremation would be best since the service would likely not happen at a church, and he did not know what religion Old Man Evans practiced, if any. A nice memorial service would be organized to take place in the chapel at the medical center so people where he worked for years, could attend. The director asked Morgan if he would be writing an obituary.

"I don't know," answered Morgan. He was unsure if he

knew enough about Old Man Evans to write one. He thought about their numerous conversations and tried to remember his age, where he grew up, where he went to college, and where else he might have worked. He was totally at a loss for knowing about his family. He hoped the human resource department at the medical center had information about his background. There must be someone else he could talk to that could fill in the gaps.

All the questions were discussed, and together they mapped out a plan of action. They needed to enter his apartment, where they might find documents with information. Mae and Morgan left the funeral home to drive to the only address they had. They found the building where he lived in senior housing. There he had a one-bedroom unit, a small and quaint home in a high-rise building with forty-five units.

The location was perfect. It was close to the bus stop, a short walking distance to a grocery store and pharmacy. The neighborhood was a mix of tiny homes, apartments, and commercial space. This building stood out as the tallest in the area, surrounded by trees and other plantings. On the lower level was a reception area, an all-purpose room where people gathered for BINGO. It had a decent living room with a sizable wide-screen television, chairs, and a couple of tables for card games. Most residents were retired. Only a few, like Evan, worked every day during the week. Morgan could not imagine him watching television during the daytime hours.

Before going to the apartment, they stopped in the management office to notify them of his passing, who they were, and why they were there. The on-duty staff person offered her condolences. She initially hesitated to let them into the apartment, but they already had a key.

"We just wanted you to know why we're here. We will empty his items from the apartment as soon as we can. Today, we're here to take inventory of his possessions."

Hopefully, that would keep staff here from rummaging through his belongings.

"Now that we know he is deceased," the manager said, "you have two weeks to remove everything from the apartment. You should also expect a refund for the rent, prorated for the month."

His apartment was filled with things strewn all over the place. It was filled with furniture: a small dining table with chairs, a double-sized bed, a dresser, and a nightstand. There was a desk with piles of papers that looked like bills and receipts. What stood out the most were storage bins and boxes piled up along the wall. Some were labeled. There had to be thirty of those things. *Maybe we will find his life's story inside,* thought Mo.

They checked to see if there was furniture they could move from his apartment to Morgan's to save some money. Bell could also use a few items too. It was hard to know where to start with the boxes. Obviously, Old Man Evans had plans for moving these items somewhere.

Morgan asked, "Where do we start?"

"Let's look at the labels first," said Aunt Mae.

They agreed only to open the boxes that were not labeled to see what types of items were in them. They'd let the stuff stay in the marked boxes for now. Eventually, they found his bank information and receipts from bills. This information would help stop the charges on those accounts. They found his social security number, date of birth, and birthplace but little regarding his family.

Mo was glad his aunt was here. She was always well organized and has probably had to do this before for a family member. He could not have done this without her support and know-how. In the boxes and the piles of paper, they discovered that Mr. Evan Deveaux was born and raised in New Orleans. He had two brothers. One was killed in Vietnam, and the other was shot on the streets of St. Louis. He was a war veteran and earned a Medal of Valor, which rested in a box among his possessions. No other family information was readily available. He had some photos, but they could not identify who was in the pictures.

Old Man Evans had earned a college degree from Xavier University in Science. He started working at what was the old hospital forty years ago. This explained why he worked at the hospital and was so revered. He had built a career as a well-known researcher. He focused most of his work on communicable and infectious diseases. A scholar by trade.

"I didn't know that," said Morgan. "He never talked about himself or boasted about all his accomplishments. He was always more interested in me and what I was doing."

There were books in piles, in boxes, and in a bookcase. Some of the books had his name as the author or contributor. Obviously, he read and wrote a lot.

All the essential information Morgan sought to enable him to write an obituary was there. There were two other items of importance with Morgan's name on them. The papers in the manila folder were about Evan Deveaux's research.

The top page had a handwritten note that read, *Morgan,*

we never talked about my work, but if you're reading this, you must pay close attention to what is written. Please do not throw away my books. They are extremely valuable. At some point, they should be donated to a library. I leave all my research notes and papers in your hands. The data is regarding a possible antibiotic to cure various bacterial infections. The research was made possible by a grant from the Stillman Foundation, based in Washington, D.C. They must be notified of my passing. But before they are contacted, reach out to Dr. Ebo at the Meharry Medical School to become the new lead researcher. He is aware of my research and is very capable of assuming this role. Whatever you do, don't let the City Medical Center grab my papers, including files, at my work office. This letter appoints you, Morgan, as the project administrative manager and provides a monthly stipend. The papers provide more details on how I envision this working.

The white business envelope on the desk was also addressed to Morgan. He picked it up and opened it. Morgan hesitated for a minute. His mind was beginning to wander. How did he know Morgan would find these letters? Why did he write to me? Why was it left in clear sight so it would be found? Finally, he tore open the envelope and began to read.

Dear Mo,

This letter is to wish you farewell. I enjoyed our talks. It was wonderful getting to know you and watching you mature. I apologize for not letting you know that I have designated you the executor of my estate—what little there is. I prefer not to cause you any alarm about my health. I have known my health was becoming a significant issue for the past year. You're a bright young man whom I admire. I saw a little of myself in you when I was your age. You may ask yourself, why me? That's easy. You were my only family, maybe not in blood but in spirit. I will wait for you on the other side to continue our conversations. Until then. (Old Man) Evan Deveaux

Morgan sat down in a chair and took a deep breath. His eyes began to tear up as he thought about the message and the loss of a dear friend. It would feel different going to work knowing Old Man Evans was no longer there. Aunt Mae came over to Morgan and placed her arm around him for comfort. She had never seen him like this before. She had no idea he had such a secret. It made her wonder if others provided her nephew with advice.

After a few more minutes, they locked the apartment, left the building, and got back in the car to drive home. Most of the day, they were busy putting all the pieces together. That kept his mind off of the loss. Now he could not think of anything else but his friend and mentor.

CHAPTER 21

Men to Men

Louis and Tre hung out at the house while everyone was busy with meetings, appointments, and shopping. Everyone expected Tre to stay home to recuperate. Louis was enjoying the rest. When these two are together, like other men of their generation, they would always talk about how it was for them growing up. Although they grew up in different places, the stories were the same.

The conversation started with a comment about today's youth.

"They don't do this or that," said Louis. "These young men are killing each other with guns. Back in the day, we fought with our hands. Only the gangster types had guns, and we didn't know them. Once the fistfight was over, no one was dead. If you got your ass kicked, your feelings might be hurt. But you were still alive. Too many of our children are dying every day from these senseless killings."

"I hear you, man," said Tre. "The worst part is they are fighting over petty things. They need to take that anger and do something productive."

Then they would shift the conversation to the lack of a

good education.

"Kids today aren't learning anything in these schools. The behavior of these unruly children result from poor parenting," said Tre. "The teachers do a poor job teaching, and the school administrators don't care. Without a good education, they won't be able to get a decent paying job."

"All of the criticism about schools never changed anything," added Louis.

Neither Louis nor Tre ever attended a PTA meeting, a school board meeting, or helped organize a community rally. Somehow, they knew what was best. Tre vividly remembered his ninth-grade teacher, Ms. Hamilton, and the principal, Mr. Jones.

"They looked out for us and encouraged us to get good grades. They understood that learning was essential. If you did well, you would graduate. Often the teachers were friends with our parents. They either went to school with them or saw each other in church. Either way, he knew to refrain from acting up in school," he recalled.

Then the topic would shift to the clothing styles of young folk.

"The girls wear clothing that hardly covers their bodies or it's too tight for the body type. All they do is attract unwanted attention," commented Louis.

"The boys wear their pants too low, showing off their colorful boxer shorts and sometimes the crack of their ass. They usually need one hand to hold the pants up from falling to their ankles. If the police were chasing them, they couldn't run away if they tried," Louis laughed.

After the men would talk and laugh about how they were

at that age. They would remember wearing colorful oversized collar shirts, platform shoes, and a huge afro. The girls wore mini-skirts showing a lot of leg. They all cut school to hang out at the mall, and did as little as possible to study because all the kids with excellent grades were not "cool." If they were fortunate enough, they had a car. Most of them rode a bike or walked everywhere they wanted to go.

"Tre," Louis interjected, "what's it like raising a girl?"

"What do you mean?" he asked.

"Did you always worry whether your daughter Jeanne was having sex with some boy who might get her pregnant?"

"Nah, man. Maybe a little. It was better not to think about it," Tre responded. "I would pay attention to who her friends were, where she said she was going, and make sure she knew we were concerned about her safety. We always had a curfew."

Tre depended on Mae to have those conversations. She could talk to her about more personal topics like birth control.

"If I gave it too much thought, I would probably not let her out of my sight. How about raising a boy?" Tre asked Louis.

"I would tell Mo, don't you come home telling me you got some girl pregnant." Louis added, "If he was having sex, he better use a condom and be safe. However, I never knew of him having a girlfriend or having a date. At times, he had me wondering if he even liked girls. We knew his closest friends, like Bell, but never paid much attention to where he went out. We didn't need to set a curfew because he never stayed out late. The boys played video games occasionally but not excessively. Mo ran track but he was not like Bell, a superstar athlete at the high school. Mo got through life on an even keel. He was a thoughtful and polite kid. We never heard negative things about him."

Louis pushed him hard about things like going to college. As parents, they wanted him to have something they did not have.

"Parents always want the best for their children."

"I understand that," Tre said. "But to be straight with you, my brother, your pushing created a greater distance in your relationship. Instead of turning to you for help or advice, he looked to others, like this man at his job, ah, Mr., ah, Old Man Evans. Since he was staying with us, I would talk to him in a firm, not demanding, voice. But I never questioned his judgment."

The men both agreed it's tough being a parent.

"Despite loving your child, there are moments when they can be upsetting," said Louis.

"I would try to teach things to Morgan, but he always reacted like I didn't know anything. Children get along better with their parents when they are younger. As they get older, it falls apart. Parents don't want them to face the same obstacles they faced, but if the parents survived, so can the children."

"I agree," said Tre.

"Today, children have it so much easier. But the world is different, making it more complex and challenging."

Tre nodded, agreeing with Louis's statement, "But every child is not the same. What might work for some does not mean it will work for all."

"Hey, do you want a drink?" asked Tre.

"Didn't the doctor tell you to lay off the alcohol?"

"I know, but one or maybe two won't hurt. It's not like I'm on any prescriptions."

"Okay, I'll take one," replied Louis. "But if anything

happens to you or Mae gets upset, don't blame me. This was your idea."

Tre went to a cabinet in the corner to pull out his favorite whiskey, a bottle of W. L. Weller 12-Year Kentucky Bourbon. Louis had never heard of it before. First, he was not a big bourbon drinker. When it came to whiskeys, he preferred scotch. Second, it's doubtful he would spend that much on a bottle of alcohol. But Tre assured him he would love it. He poured a little into a glass over ice. Louis took a sniff and almost got high from the fumes. He agreed. It had a smooth texture, and after a few sips, his palate got used to the high potency.

"I used to watch my dad and granddad sit around and drink that moonshine made by one of the neighbors," Tre said.

"There was not much for them to do around here. It's not like up north with nightclubs or nice restaurants to impress your date. When you got old enough and able to handle your liquor, you joined the other men."

By the afternoon, Bell and Mo arrived to join the conversation. They primarily shared the stories of the day. Mo talked about what he found in the apartment. The men each stated how much work is entailed but how fortunate he is to have received this unexpected inheritance.

"If you receive some money, invest as much as possible," said Louis.

Tre advised, "As you get older, you begin to understand how much you need if you're able to retire or help cover medical bills. Are there many belongings to sort through to either toss or give to Goodwill?"

"Too much stuff," replied Mo.

"I'll help you move it," Bell inserted.

"Thanks. I need all the help I can get. It's hard to paint a picture of how much stuff Old Man Evans had in that small apartment. I was especially surprised by the volume of books in the bookcase and piled three to four feet high on the floor. It was hard to imagine him reading all those books."

Old Man Evans was once a college professor. Morgan had no idea what he taught, but from the looks of everything, it must have been some area in science. He did learn more about the man and his work in infectious diseases.

Morgan turned and looked at Uncle Tre.

"I almost forgot to ask you, How are you feeling? Are you getting the needed rest, or is my dad keeping you from sleeping?"

"I'm feeling pretty good. Ready to return to work."

"Do they know what's wrong? Did the doctor give you any meds?" Mo asked.

He watched Tre sipping on his glass of whiskey, knowing that alcohol was not a part of his treatment. The doctors at the hospital did not prescribe any medications but advised him to see his primary care doctor as soon as possible. He had an appointment with Dr. Troy for the next day. All the men knew Tre was probably not doing well but would not admit it.

Bell wanted to share what he had been doing. He told his story of meeting Tricia, the girl at the apartments, and her boyfriend. The guys all laughed. Bell did not find it all that funny.

"She's a big tease," Bell said.

"That's not your problem. Her boyfriend needs to worry about that," said Louis.

"Hey, young man, we've all been there. Girls like to flirt to see how you'll react. She'll come around again when the boyfriend is not there. The question is, how will you respond?"

Bell was still pouting about them laughing at him. He now wished he had not told them. It's not like he liked this person. He was just glad to meet someone new.

"Mo, I advise you to stay clear of them and don't mess up the good thing you have with your girl," said Bell.

Tre said, "That's good advice."

Then Mae walked into the room and immediately noticed the empty glasses on the coffee table.

"Tre, have you been drinking? You know the doctor told you to take a break."

"I did for a couple of days," replied Tre.

"Louis, I'm holding you responsible. Tre doesn't know any better. I expected you to watch him and prevent him from ending up back in the medical center. You men are more than any woman can handle. Boys, don't be like these old men," Mae said as she exited the living room. Mae left the room shaking her head.

"I knew you would get me in trouble," said Louis.

Changing the topic, Tre asked, "So, who do we like this weekend, the Steelers or the Browns?"

The guys carried on for an hour talking about football. They debated which team was better, which players were better, and who would be in the playoffs. They each took turns saying, I'll bet ya. None of the bets were written down. No money was thrown on the table. Regardless, that would not stop Uncle T from letting you know if he won.

Louis turned his head. He looked at Morgan with admiration, knowing he would be okay. It was a good thing that Bell was also here. Now he had an old friend to be there to hang out with. He was even more pleased that he had a good job, one where he was respected.

"Mo," said Louis, "I'm sure your mom was taking care of business with KeTani to purchase what was needed for the apartment. How else can I help you?"

Morgan was not sure what he might be referring to. He had not been asked that question before by his dad. He did not believe there was anything he wanted to ask at this time. Morgan's mind was focused on planning a memorial service. He had Aunt Mae helping with those arrangements. Morgan let his dad know he was glad he was here. He enjoyed the time they've spent together.

Louis said, "Morgan, I'm sorry if I pushed you too hard and made you feel it would be better to leave home. I should have spent more time with you, getting to know what you liked to do. Instead, I was fixed on you doing what I wanted you to do, such as going to college. I now know that what I had hoped for you was not necessarily the best for you. Keep doing what you do. I'm sure you'll be okay." Morgan gave him an affirming nod.

Morgan thanked his dad for the information in the black pouch. There, Morgan found his birth certificate and official Social Security Card. There was a photo of Morgan with his parents when he was five and a picture of him at high school graduation. There were a few other items, but the most prominent document was the Fidelity account information. His parents saved these funds for him to attend college, but they were never used. There was a note attached to the document. It read:

Use this to continue your education or start a business. Love you, Mom & Dad.

It was truly an unexpected gift.

The guys continued to talk late into the evening. Mae and Maggie were in the kitchen. Morgan finally slipped away to give KeTani a call.

"Hey, beautiful," Mo said.

KeTani replied, as always, "Hi, handsome."

"Sorry we didn't see each other today. If your day was anything like mine, it was busy. Mom shared information about the day you had together. It sounds like it was productive."

"It was busy, but we bought the necessary items for the apartment."

"The furniture will be delivered either tomorrow or on the weekend. One of us will need to be there to receive it. I've also set up all of our utilities. I hope you're ready."

Morgan shared his experience at the lawyer's office and Old Man Evan's apartment. He then read the letter, and the note he found in the apartment addressed to him. He was still shocked and saddened by the circumstances. Morgan talked more about the responsibility that had been placed on him unexpectedly. This was more than he could have ever have imagined.

"You'll do fine," said KeTani. "And, I got your back."

After another thirty minutes of conversation, they agreed to meet at their new apartment around 10:00 AM.

Morgan just sat for a few minutes thinking about her, and then it hit him. To make it a scarier scenario, he would be living with a roommate, his girlfriend. He would need to learn how to share things. He would no longer be the center of attention like an only child. It would be all about us. Morgan and KeTani got along with each other. They have similar interests when it came to socially going out. The challenge would be for him to find space when it felt he needed some privacy. He had never thought about those things before now.

He was overjoyed to have someone he could call his girlfriend. And she was not only amazingly beautiful but someone he genuinely loved. That feeling of being in love and being loved was new. Morgan's feelings for her were strong. There was this undeniable emotional connection they had for each other. He could not stop thinking of her when they were not together. Living together would bring them closer. He was not sure if he would get tired of seeing her. KeTani was fabulous at making him feel loved. The way she looked at him and expressed her feelings of affection. They now would have more time to be more intimate. Time would tell whether they made the right decision.

CHAPTER 22

Thursday Night

Everyone was tired and ready to call it a day when they noticed Tre slumped in his chair. They assumed he fell asleep as he usually did while watching television. Aunt Mae called out to him, but he didn't move.

"Tre! Get up and go to bed. Go on now," she shouted.

Then, she went over to shake him to get him going. He grumbled a few words as if to say he heard her and stop bothering him simultaneously. Tre stood up and took a few steps but then collapsed. His legs just gave out from under him. On the way down, he bumped his head on the coffee table, which caused a gash just above his right eye. Blood was streaming out and getting all over the floor and on his clothes.

Stunned by what had happened, they rushed over to pick him up. He was mostly unconscious. As he gained consciousness, Tre did not know where he was or what he was doing. Morgan immediately called 911 to have an ambulance take him back to the medical center.

His training taught him to seek proper medical care. Too many people think they know what to do after watching television shows. Morgan would not take that chance. He had enough experience at the medical center to temporarily patch up a wound and stop it from bleeding until the EMS team arrived. Morgan knew Uncle Tre needed professional help beyond patching up the cut.

Aunt Mae panicked, screaming, "I knew it! I knew it!"

Everyone else did not know what she was talking about. Was it the drinking or not staying in bed to get rest? Was she blaming the doctor for allowing him to be discharged without determining what caused him to faint? Was he ignoring some serious medical issue that none of us knew about? What did she know? Finally, the ambulance arrived outside. They rushed in, placed him on a stretcher, placed an oxygen mask over his mouth, and checked his pulse. Within minutes, they drove off as quickly as they could.

Aunt Mae and Maggie got in the car to drive to the medical center to be with Tre in the ER. They were both thinking, this is going to be another long night.

"He should have never been discharged until it was clear what caused him to fall at work," said Mae. "Now he will need stitches and possibly has a concussion." As they were driving, Mae shared her fear.

"All the men in his family died early from a heart attack, diabetes, or stroke. None of them took care of their health through proper diets and exercise. It was just a matter of time for Tre. This time, we will ask them to keep him until a diagnosis has been made and he receives prescriptions to address the problems." Mae was hoping it would be a warning to Tre that he had been given a second chance.

"Tre is not an excessive drinker, but he has one or two every day, more than the doctors recommend," Mae continued. "He never goes for a walk. He eats a lot of junk food and rejects vegetables other than collard greens." She laughed and said, "He can't resist my cooking, especially the greens. I need to reduce the fat and salt I use in cooking."

At one point, his doctor prescribed meds for his high blood pressure. She thinks he just stopped taking them for no reason. He felt good and no longer felt the need to take the meds. Tre likes to wait until he is in severe pain before he takes his health seriously. Lord knows she worried about him every moment of the day.

Louis, Bell, and Morgan sat quietly back at the house, wondering what they could have done. He was, by default, under their watch, if not their care. None of them stopped him from drinking, and Louis joined in.

"I should have stopped him from drinking."

He was told not to drink. One drink was too many. None of them watched him closely as he drifted off to sleep. Morgan had seen him fall asleep almost every night in front of the television. It never crossed his mind that maybe something would be wrong this time.

Morgan asked, "Are we responsible for what just happened?"

Bell said, "Am I my brother's keeper? Genesis 4:1-9." Morgan turned to look at Bell, not expecting him to recite a Bible verse.

Louis said, "That passage is more about jealousy. Isn't it?"

Bell replied, "It's also about providing for the well-being of others."

"In that case, I guess we failed to do our job," Morgan said.

They all just hung their heads and felt a little guilty.

"Everything we experience has a reason," Bell again spoke

up. "We learn from our mistakes and bear the consequences of our decisions. That's what growing older means, isn't it, Mr. Ordell?"

Morgan and Louis turned to look at Bell, wondering where he learned these nuggets of wisdom.

"You're right. And I have made my share of mistakes and bad decisions," Louis replied. "It's all part of growing up."

"Dad, all through high school, you always emphasized what it takes to become a man." Louis told Morgan when a man transitions from boyhood to adulthood, he becomes more responsible for himself and those around him.

"A man learns how to make wise choices for himself, his friends, and his family. He is respectful of others, especially women and the elderly, but kind and generous to those in need."

Louis wanted Morgan to understand that he was concerned with his future. He wanted him to know that you hope the best for your child.

Morgan interrupted, "There you go again about me not attending college. Everyone does not do that. There are other ways to make a living. It's also not too late for me to pursue a degree."

"We respect your decision and see you've done well." Louis acknowledged getting the apartment and finding a lovely young lady as examples. He further applauded him on his job with a future career ahead of him.

"You demonstrated what it means to be 'my brother's keeper,'" inserted Bell.

"We each mature at our own pace. Some males never grow up," Louis added.

"I'm happy to hear you feel that way now," said Mo. "But I have always felt you were never pleased with my choices."

"I remember when the decision was made to move in with Tre and Mae. I knew at that moment that things would be okay."

"How's that?"

"For you to decide to move anywhere was to not sit idly by staying at home with us," stated Louis. "Plus, we wanted to be empty nesters, a goal of every parent after raising a child," trying to bring a little levity into the conversation.

"Was I that bad or difficult?" asked Morgan.

"No, son. Not at all."

"Bell, did your family bug you about going to college?" asked Morgan.

"They didn't need to. I was destined to play football. Neither my parents nor my brother ever attended college. But they were all aware of my being recruited to play football. Now, they must all be upset with me because I will not be in the NFL making lots of money and buying them a new house like so many have done. Maybe one of these days, I will try to return to get a degree. Before, I didn't have a clue about what I'd study. Right now, I'm satisfied just to have a job."

"Are you planning to stay here longer with Uncle T hospitalized? Aunt Mae might still need your help," Morgan asked.

"No, son," Louis replied. "After tonight, I'm sure she does not need my help. I suspect we will leave Saturday morning. I've got to get back to work. Let's wait and see what your mom wants to do. We also made this trip to see you and help you move into an apartment. We will know better tomorrow. We can each take turns visiting Tre. Laying in a bed at the hospital is not fun, especially when you don't feel sick."

"If you two want to call it a night, that's okay," said Louis.

He offered to stay awake until the women returned home. Who knows how long that might take? He wished them a good night's sleep and told them not to worry about Uncle T. He'll recover and return home soon. Bell and Morgan walked upstairs as suggested. Both were feeling tired yet anxious about what had happened. Tomorrow they were both heading to the apartment to begin the moving-in process. Arrangements had been made to deliver boxes to pack up Old Man Evan's apartment. They needed to be there to receive the items and ensure the electricity was turned on. All of the books and papers were coming too and would take up a lot of space in the second bedroom/office.

CHAPTER 23

End of the Week

Morgan and Bell drove over to Grace Gardens together. As planned, Morgan would meet KeTani there. His mom and dad would be with Aunt Mae all day, by her side at the medical center and home. They were ready to deal with whatever news they received from the doctor about Uncle T.

Morgan looked back on this week and thought about everything that had happened. Other than the health issues Uncle T was experiencing, his life had definitely changed for the better. At the top of the list was his initial goal to move into an apartment. Today was Friday, and Morgan and KeTani declared the as day one in their apartment. They were finally moving in after a week of distractions. The place looked clean and ready for some personal touches. KeTani's car was filled with kitchenware and linens that needed to be unloaded. They all made several trips carrying the boxes from the car to the empty space. Later, when the trucks arrive, there will be more to lift, carry and move around. Right now, there were no chairs to sit on, just boxes.

Morgan looked across the living room at his girlfriend. This was a new experience for him. He was still determining what it meant and what he must do. But he was sure that it felt good. His parents, uncle, and aunt were the only examples of how it might look. Both were married. None of the Watchmen crew were ever in steady relationships in high school. He was wondering whether this relationship would last a long time. Are they required to make joint decisions? Must he tell her everywhere he goes? Will she do the same? Morgan was trying to think about KeTani's expectations of him. She took charge of setting up the apartment, which he appreciated since he did not know what to do. Is this a glimpse into her being in charge? Regardless, he now had a partner in his life that should make things easier.

Bell left them at their apartment to go to his unit and begin the same process, except he was alone. Being alone was not a concerning factor. He considered his situation an improvement over where he was last week. He was no longer homeless or jobless. He also cherished the moment that Morgan found him on the corner. From his perspective, "If it were not for the grace of God," he might still be standing on the corner. Morgan and Bell were reunited. By coincidence, they would live in the same apartment complex. Bell was busy trying to set up his apartment with furniture and household items. He had all the stuff left behind by the previous tenant. He also had items contributed by Old Man Evans that Morgan decided to give him to save him some money. He now had pots and pans, cooking utensils, dishes, bowls, glassware, a few pieces of furniture, and much more.

As he was getting things set up, he heard a knock on the door. He immediately thought it was Morgan. He dreaded the thought that the police were looking for him again. Instead, it was the Three Ts. This time, Tina spoke.

"Hi."

Bell just stood there waiting to hear what she had to say. They felt sorry for what happened the other day when he came to the party.

"Jerrold, the guy who answered the door, should not have done that."

Bell shrugged his shoulders. He was okay. He wouldn't make that mistake again. He asked them how he could help them, being polite. He also wanted them to know that he does not officially start working there until Monday. His goal was to keep it strictly business.

"So, whatever it is, will have to wait," Bell said. Tina tried to be the peacemaker. She again expressed their apologies.

"Tricia should have come to the door. Instead, she told Jerrold it was okay to let you in. We found out later that he told you to leave. He is not her boyfriend."

Bell asked, "Why would he say he's her boyfriend if he wasn't?"

"He thinks of himself as our protector. He's always talking about keeping unwanted men away," Tina replied.

"You need protection?"

"No, not really. But you never know."

Tricia then handed him a bottle of wine. She asked that he please accept it from all three of them as a welcome gift. They hoped he would accept future invitations to their parties. Bell said thank you, even though he didn't care much for wine. He didn't know one wine from another, red or white. He mostly drank beer or whiskey. He was thoroughly surprised, and for the moment, it left him feeling better about the 3Ts. He was not ready to completely forgive them. He was glad they explained what happened but was reminded to stay focused on the job and not spend time socializing with the residents.

Tricia asked if he would come to the next party. She promised him a good time. He was not sure he would, and if her friends were anything like Jerrold, it might not be fun. He appreciated the peace offering though.

It felt like a college prank, and he was the butt of the joke. He really wanted Jerrold to offer an apology. They left, and Bell just shook his head. He was curious to know if they were being honest. They realized he would take his time to address the problem when they needed him to respond to a maintenance issue.

When Bell caught up with Morgan and KeTani later that afternoon, he brought over the bottle of wine. They wanted to know where he got it. He shared the story with them. They were initially shocked but later found it humorous.

"Let's be happy these ladies weren't as bad as they appeared," Morgan said. "Grab a few glasses, and let's toast to celebrate moving in and our continued friendship."

KeTani told them, "Let what happened be a warning. Those ladies are trouble."

Morgan did not need any more reminders. Bell, however, was still intrigued.

***

The family members agreed to take turns visiting Tre in the hospital. It was time for Morgan to drop in. The feeling was to provide company and to observe if the medical staff was taking good care of him. As usual, they were administering test after test to determine the problem. The doctor finally concluded that Uncle T had a minor stroke. It appears he might have had some blood clots in his leg. There was no specific cause, but rather a list of preventative measures for him, starting with no alcoholic beverages. That's almost like taking away someone's candy or chocolate. It's hard to imagine him living without it.

They wanted him to remain at the hospital for at least another day before he would be discharged again. He was also advised to start some form of cardio exercise. Aunt Mae planned to put him on a diet of healthier foods and poured out the alcohol. He had fifteen stitches to close up the gash over his eye. It was uncertain if or when he might return to work. The next few weeks of rest and doctor's appointments would determine the necessary action. In the days ahead, Aunt Mae would be left caring for Uncle T. All her house guests from the past few days would have moved on. Watching over Tre will be easier for her to manage with no other family around to tend to things at home while spending hours at the medical center. The night before, getting him into a private room took hours. Once he got settled and asleep, the family went back home to get some rest.

Suddenly, Morgan thought, *what if Uncle T could not return to work?* What if he needed help with things around the house? Was this a reason why he should not move to the apartment? Would Aunt Mae ask him to stay if she needed him to? How could he fulfill his dreams if other things got in the way? It would not be fair. *Aunt Mae would not do that to me.* He continued to think. She would want him to move forward with his life.

Aunt Mae told us she called Jeanne. She and her family lived just a few hours away. She did not feel it necessary to contact her earlier in the week. This time she felt required to call. Jeanne decided to arrive on Sunday and provide Aunt Mae with some company. She would spend time at the hospital visiting with her dad. Together they might be able to convince Tre to take the doctor's recommendations seriously. He was too young to retire from work. He had also worked for the county government long enough that it would not be a good idea to walk away from the pension plan too early.

Morgan took the time to tell Aunt Mae how much he appreciated the past four years in their home.

"I'll come by weekly to take care of the lawn until Uncle T is ready to take over. I'm sure he'll miss being outside to care for his property."

Morgan said he would also care for his car. Morgan stated with a big smile on his face. He quietly prayed he would get to drive his car as often as he liked.

He understood he would not be where he was without them letting him live there while he got his shit together.

Morgan's parents departed on Saturday. Besides Tre's unfortunate dilemma, spending time with their son and learning how well he was doing was great. They got to meet KeTani and her parents. The sisters, Mae and Maggie, got caught up on things. They all agreed not to let so many months go by without a visit. Maggie was not pleased departing her sister's side before Tre returned home. She would turn around in a heartbeat and come right back. Morgan and his parents said their goodbyes. Morgan promised to travel home in six months to visit. By then, Bell would want to see his parents too. On that trip home they would try to connect with Tyler and Cory.

Bell would keep his secrets to himself. The past weeks, he had a few nightmares to forget. But mostly, he was getting his life back on track. He was embarrassed about losing his job. Living on the street and in a shelter was hell. The things he saw and witnessed were not to be shared with anyone, most of all not with Morgan. The unfortunate hit-and-run accident will not be easily forgotten.

In the weeks ahead, Morgan planned a memorial service to recognize Old Man Evans's life. The number of staff and friends that attended filled the chapel. The medical center director spoke and the hospital chaplain offered the eulogy. There were no family members, just a few science colleagues and residents from senior housing.

Morgan was still unsure how much he would inherit, but whatever the amount, it would help financially. He now had a new role as an administrator for Dr. Deveaux's research project. He wore this like a badge of honor. As he reminisced about his mentor, he recalled him saying, "I have but one goal in life, and that is to always keep my dignity and spirits high above my head."

He never judged you by what you did or where you came from. He treated everyone the same. He would tell Morgan to become a man of values. Now it's Morgan's time.

CHAPTER 24

Six Months Later

It's a Friday night, and the end of another busy work week had finally arrived. Tonight would be a good time to stop at Jimmie's, the neighborhood bar. Morgan had heard so much about this place a long time ago but never wanted to go by himself. Now he had lots of friends to join him, starting with KeTani and Bell. She also invited her former roommates to join them. The place had an extended bar area, tables and chairs for about eighty people, and an excellent DJ playing the latest party music. However, the open space was inadequate for dancing, which did not prevent people from getting up to dance. The food was an essential item, nothing fancy, yet good tasting. If you go early, the noise level was low enough for conversation.

The hostess found a table for six. KeTani and Morgan took a seat. Until the others arrived, they did some people-watching, a favorite sport. They commented on the array of styles, clothing, and hair, which was a sight to behold in that particular crowd. The waitress finally came over and asked if they wanted a drink. They both ordered mixed cocktails. She asked for IDs to prove they were legally old enough to drink.

Seeing so many beautiful Black people enjoying a night out was nice. Morgan reflected on his time in Memphis and could not believe he had missed out on all this. Finally, Jasmin and Jackie arrived, and they joined them at the table.

"Hey, ladies," Morgan greeted them.

"Hey, Mo," they responded. Shortly after, Bell arrived with Tricia. Not too long after that initial mix-up, they finally forgave each other and slowly became close friends.

They were all talking, laughing, having fun, and enjoying the beginning of the weekend. Morgan only recognized a few other people he knew and met at Jimmie's. Most of the folk there were new faces, some a little older. That didn't matter. They had their own little party at the table.

Morgan celebrated all the great things happening in this new adult life. This was the most fun Morgan had at a club since his move south. He was with friends, old and new. The atmosphere was exciting, and he was feeling better about himself. Life was good! Bell ordered a bottle of champagne so he could deliver a celebratory toast. Morgan was wondering where Bell got the money to order a bottle of champagne. Bell told him not to worry. He jokingly said he stole it from the back of the bar.

"Don't worry about it, my friend. I got this."

"Here's to my dearest friend, Morgan, and his lovely girlfriend, KeTani. After six months, they are still living together in the apartment and have not attempted to kill each other." Everyone laughed.

Jasmin jumped in and said, "Cheers to getting KeTani out of our apartment. She was beginning to be annoying, talking about Mo this and Mo that. We were getting tired of hearing about how nice he is."

Again, they all laughed. KeTani was embarrassed, and Morgan smiled when he looked at her.

Morgan spoke up and acknowledged his renewed friendship with Bell, who had an apartment of his own and a job.

"May the friendship continue for a long time," said Morgan. Morgan also offered cheers to his mentor, Dr. Evan Deveaux, whom he no longer referred to as Old Man Evans. "May he rest in peace."

Several other patrons looked over at their group. They all gave them a stare as if to say, why are you here, and who are you? Morgan momentarily thought someone would ask them to leave because they were making too much noise. But as more and more people came in, they began blending into the fabric. Things got noisier by 9 PM. A couple of drinks later, the place started filling up.

KeTani and Morgan got up to dance, and Bell danced with Tricia. That left the J girls at the table. The music was soulful and great for embracing your partner without leaving space between the bodies. Morgan took his hands and caressed KeTani's back, then placed them in the small of her back. She had her hands around his shoulders and his neck. Both were humming to the music and keeping time. For a moment, it was as if nobody else was in the club, just the two of them dancing to a slow jam. They stood there when the music finally stopped, hoping another slow song would follow. They gazed into each other's eyes as if to say, don't stop. He gave her a long and passionate kiss that neither one wanted to stop. But the DJ played a dance track and the energy shifted in the club.

Everybody, seemed to be having fun. The group hung out there until well after midnight.

Tomorrow, like they do every Saturday, Morgan and KeTani would drive over to visit with Aunt Mae and Uncle T. Since his last medical incident, he was persuaded to retire. Going to work every day kept him active. But the stress was more than he could withstand. Now he sits often and sometimes goes outside to tend to his yard, the grass, bushes, leaves, and weeds. Uncle T had to stop drinking, but he sneaks a little taste when he can. His car rarely leaves the house, but that does not stop him from keeping it shining on the outside and meticulously clean inside. Aunt Mae spends more time at church these days, helping wherever and whenever possible. Anything to make sure she does not sit around worrying about her husband.

Morgan had found happiness in his relationships with KeTani, his best-friend Bell, and his family. Morgan successfully got the apartment and plans to attend college next year to further his education. He has a purpose to manage a scientific research project.

Epilogue

The characters in this book are fictional. This is not a true story but rather a collage or tapestry of stories woven together. Morgan's story is just one person's experience transitioning from youth to adulthood. There's no timetable or specific age when this should occur. For many people, their life will depend on the surrounding environment, the blending of unintended circumstances with personal decisions.

Life changes often begin with influences from your immediate family and relationships with friends. It is also impacted by the many individuals entering your life and the various professional and social acquaintances that can lift you up.

Most of us can identify at least one or more mentors that crossed our path. Their guidance can help you navigate over, around, or through challenges. Learning who you can trust is critical. Sometimes it is what you learn from your mistakes and your negative experiences. If you have not figured it out yet, it's nearly impossible not to have a setback or make a mistake.

It's Time for Mo tells a story about a young man finally reaching the point where he is ready to become an adult. What defines adulthood will also be different for each person. For Morgan, it was not living at home or under the roof of a family member. He failed to recognize that adulthood was also defined by his employment and his unwavering character to be generous.

He grappled with the definition of manhood. As a Black man, our experiences in this society can be different. For a mother, how do you raise a son and teach him how to be a man? As a mentor, how do you provide guidance that helps a person grow into the man they are to become? I'm hoping this story sheds some light on these questions.

My message to young men is this. The key is to keep going. Know that you have angels that you might not visibly see but who look out for you. It's better to make your own decision regarding the life you wish to live. Others cannot possibly sense what's in your heart and mind. Don't give up on your dream(s). Dare to take thoughtful risks, understanding that everything requires hard work. Nothing is just handed to you. Give it time and look to yourself for the answers to what you must change.

www.ingramcontent.com/pod-product-compliance
Lightning Source LLC
Chambersburg PA
CBHW010544170726
48285CB00008B/2738